Charles Baxter

THROUGH THE SAFETY NET

Charles Baxter lives in Ann Arbor and teaches at the University of Michigan. He is the author of three previous collections of stories, *Harmony of the World*, *Believers*, and *A Relative Stranger*, and two novels, *First Light* and *Shadow Play*.

Charles Baxter

➤✦

THROUGH THE SAFETY NET

STORIES

VINTAGE CONTEMPORARIES

VINTAGE BOOKS

A DIVISION OF RANDOM HOUSE, INC.

NEW YORK

For Tom, Lew, and Daniel Baxter
and in memory of Dennis Turner

FIRST VINTAGE CONTEMPORARIES EDITION, OCTOBER 1998

Copyright © 1985 by Charles Baxter

The writing of these stories was supported by grants from the National Endowment
of the Arts and the Wayne State Fund.

Some of the stories in this book appeared originally in the following periodicals:
Black Warrior Review, "Winter Journey"; *Epoch*, "Gryphon"; *Michigan Quarterly*,
"A Late Sunday Afternoon by the Huron"; *Stand*, "Cataract"; *Tendril*, "Media
Event"and "Surprised by Joy"; and *Twilight Zone*, "Through the Safety Net."

Grateful acknowledgment is made to New Directions Publishing Corporation for
permission to reprint eight lines from "Seurat's Sunday Afternoon Along the Seine,"
from Delmore Schwartz, *Selected Poems: Summer Knowledge*.
Copyright © 1959 by Delmore Schwartz.

Library of Congress Cataloging-in-Publication Data

Baxter, Charles, 1947–
Through the safety net : stories / by Charles Baxter. —1st Vintage contemporaries ed.
p.   cm.
Contents: Stained glass—Winter journey—Saul and Patsy are getting comfortable in
Michigan—Media event—Surprised by joy—Talk show—Cataract—The eleventh
floor—Gryphon—Through the safety net—A late Sunday afternoon by the Huron.
ISBN 0-679-77649-4
1. United States—Social life and customs—20th century—Fiction.
2. Middle class—United States—Fiction. I. Title.
PS3552.A854T4   1998
813'.54—dc21   98-26445
CIP

Author photograph © Martha Baxter

Random House Web address: www.randomhouse.com

Printed in the United States of America
10 9 8 7 6 5 4 3 2 1

Contents

Stained Glass

She thought he was a decent enough man until she tried to break up with him. They were sitting at the back of a restaurant drinking decaffeinated coffee; she was gesturing with her hands and saying that this *thing*, their relationship, wasn't going anywhere and that he knew it. His hands lay flat in his lap as he listened to her, and his blue eyes never moved in his bland pudgy face. When he didn't respond to what she had said, she stood up. He reached out for her arm, missed it, and knocked over his water glass. It was nearly empty, and only the ice cubes spilled out on the tablecloth, sliding in her direction. She looked at him, paid for her half of the bill, and walked out to her Toyota. She was turning the key in the ignition when, hearing something, she looked to her left at the window and saw his hand pressed flat against it. Then the fingernails began scrabbling against the glass. She had already pressed down the lock. She heard his voice coming in gasping explosive waves from behind his hand. Only three of his words were audible: " . . . can't . . . do . . . this." She shifted the Toyota into first gear, released the clutch, and drove out of the parking lot, seeing him, slouched and coiled, receding in the rearview mirror.

When she arrived home the following day, she found inside the building, at the door of her apartment, a dozen long-stemmed red roses wrapped in bright-green florist tissue paper. She opened the note.

Dear Donna,

Please excuse my rage.
You ARE these roses. They ARE you,
but the red IS the red of MY heart.
Try to think again of me. Try to
bleed as I am bleeding.

Love, Bobby

After considering the matter, she called the apartment manager and asked for a new Segal lock on the door. He grumbled but said he'd get it done eventually, only it'd be quicker if *she* did it. In the yellow pages she found a listing for Thomas Grobowski, an all-night locksmith, who arrived within the hour and was finished by nine-thirty. He was a bald, middle-aged man who hummed Chopin while he made measurements and tested screws. He said, "Break up with someone?" Then, after he scanned her face, he said, "I get so many jobs like this, this time of night, from nice people. People just like you." He shook his head and whistled.

On her desk at the office the next morning were two embossed boxes of chocolates, sent by Candygram. The first box contained one pound of chocolate-covered cherries, and the second box, weighing two pounds, was an assortment: marshmallow creams, chocolate-covered solid caramel, semisweet layered chocolate, pieces with nougat or jellied fruit inside, and chocolate-covered cashews and peanuts. Once again there was a note on green stationery tucked inside a tiny envelope. She didn't read it. During her coffee break she walked down the carpeted fluorescent corridor with both boxes held in front of her, gave one to a secretary she knew with three children, and left the two-pound box with the typing pool.

At home, she could hear the telephone jangling as she turned the shiny key in the new lock. As soon as she answered, he began talking rapidly, with shallow breaths, almost a drugged voice, but faster than she'd ever heard him: a voice transformed by insomnia. "I love you," he said, first thing. "Don't you know that? Are you crazy? Did you read my notes? Did you eat the candy? I chose that candy *with you in mind.* Have you thought about the talks we used to have? Summer-night talks? Bedtime talks? *I've* thought about them. How about the trip to Mexico we planned? Uxmal and those other ruins. Donna, right now I feel like I'm dying. I feel like I'm already dead. You can't just put an end to what we had to-gether, not just like that." She heard him snapping his fingers. "I'm here at work and I'm going nuts with these customers. I can't believe you and I aren't a team anymore, especially after you *said* we were a team."

She could hear the sound of electronic cash registers in the background at Crazy Benny's Auto Parts, where he was the manager and had a semiprivate office, with a doorway but no door. She was beginning to count to ten.

"Remember how we used to lie in bed early? We made wishes before the sun came up. Once you wished you had gone to veterinarian school. I wished I had floated in the Great Salt Lake. Remember how we'd sit in restaurants? We made up stories about the people we saw. Remember how I tuned your car, and fixed the carburetor in January? Damn it, Donna, are you listening to me? *Doesn't my love mean anything to you?* We had problems. Okay, everyone has problems. But what about New Year's Eve? I can tell you exactly where we were standing in Susan and Randy's living room when we kissed. I know how long that kiss was. One minute and ten seconds. And what about the glass I gave you? Jesus, I feel so lousy that I could . . . I don't know. I could . . . "

She had reached ten. She hung up on him.

She walked over to her dining-room table and sat with a cup of warm coffee between her hands. She glanced toward the ceiling. Above her was the stained-glass mock-Tiffany chandelier Bobby had made in his basement. The bulb threw out irregular blue, green, and maroon geometric shapes onto the upper walls. Bobby's basement was full of Tiffany chandeliers, theme windows, block glass ashtrays, pastel-blue cigarette boxes, clocks, planters, and animal-motif decorative mirrors he had made with stained glass and had tried to sell at local art fairs. Hour by hour he sat on his white Naugahyde stool making these things. The unsold products of his time were stashed neatly on the north, south, and east walls in his basement on shelves, each one catalogued with a white tag, an inventory number, a first asking price, a second asking price in code, and the names of the fairs where it had been displayed. With all these objects filling up space in the basement, there was little room for Bobby to store new ones. He had given her the chandelier and a vanity mirror for her bedroom. Their style was earnest Art Deco, without flair or humor. She decided to leave them up for the time being.

During the next week, she found three letters each day from him waiting for her in the mailbox, eighteen letters for the whole week. She threw most of the envelopes unopened into the wastebasket, but when she did open one of them she found a poem inside. A poem from Bobby! The idea of Bobby writing a poem gave her a queer feeling. She read the first six lines.

> I can hear the harvest moon talking to me and
> It's saying that it knows all about
> Lovers, and honey that's us, and the moon is
> Angry that you are stopping such
> A good thing, the fighting mad moon says Hey Donna
> Get back together with Bobby, he can't stand

She didn't read any more. Her shaking hand blurred the print. She carried the letter by its torn corner to the kitchen, where she dropped it in the pantry flip-up garbage can. At least he wasn't making any phone calls; she had changed the number on him.

The next morning when she pulled the curtains in the living room, there he was, staring up at her from the apartment courtyard. Her right hand reached instinctively up to her mouth. Bobby was the picture of calm: his arms were folded over his chest, and on his face was the faintest of smiles. She yanked the curtains shut. Then she sat down and thought heavily of what she was going to do. Bobby might stand there all day. He was capable of it: his hobby required terrible patience. After she had tried to drink a glass of orange juice and was ready to leave for work, she knocked at the door of the couple upstairs, the Seaforths. Mrs. Seaforth came to the door in her pink bathrobe and fuzzy bedroom slippers. "There's a man outside the building," Donna said. "An ex-boyfriend of mine. He's just standing there. He's upset and angry at me. I don't want to call the police or the security people. I just wondered . . . I just wondered if you or Mr. Seaforth could walk me out to my car."

She realized that she was embarrassed saying these things, and she was angry that she was embarrassed.

Mrs. Seaforth, who was sixty, and a fan of soap operas, looked at her with an unreadable expression. When Donna was finished speaking, Mrs. Seaforth invited her in while she went to get her husband. In five minutes the couple were both dressed, and they walked Donna down to her car, Mr. Seaforth on her left, Mrs. Seaforth on her right.

"What will you do about this fellow?" Mr. Seaforth asked on the stairs. "We'll help you all we can, but we can't walk you to your car every morning. We sleep late. I think you should call the police. They take care of nuisances. That's their job."

They looked for Bobby, who was nowhere in sight.

"I don't know what I'll do," Donna said, unlocking her Toyota, which had a note squeezed in under the right rear tire. "I have to think about it." She backed up over the note, and when the Seaforths had turned around and were walking toward the front entry, she stopped the car, picked up the folded paper with tire tracks on it, and threw it into the dumpster.

At lunchtime she told the story of the last week to two women, Lila and Nadine. Lila was large-boned; in the office her heroic stature commanded attention, and, unlike Nadine, she enjoyed giving orders. "Of course you can call the police," she said, biting into a carrot, "but that won't get you far. They'll round up the usual excuses, ask you if he's assaulted you, and when you say no, well, that's it."

Nadine perked up. She touched her painted fingernails to her forehead. "Do you have any old boyfriends you could invite in for a couple of weeks?" At this suggestion, Lila raised her eyebrows and began to chew faster. "If you don't," Nadine continued, "I do. Some nice guys. If he sees you with them, he'll give up." Nadine was a beauty; often in the morning she had a drowsy look.

"I don't want that," Donna said. "I don't want another man fixing this."

"Why?" Nadine asked. Lila was nodding.

"This is political. What he's doing to me is political. You don't solve a man with another man. I have to do it some other way."

Lila sat back for a moment, gripping a piece of celery. At last she said, "Okay, listen. I think I've got it. Listen to this."

At the office he couldn't reach her because the secretaries had been warned, but somehow he obtained her new home phone number, and that night he called. "I'm much calmer now," he said. "Donna, are you listening? *I'm much calmer.*

I've got this thing under control." He waited, then said, "I love you, don't you understand that?" Now he was shouting. "Don't you know what in the goddamn hell love is?"

At once Donna handed the phone to Lila, who, according to her own plan, was there in the room with her. "All right, who is this?" Lila asked. "Who are you?"

After a five-second silence, he said, "What? Who is this?"

"This is Lila."

"Who's Lila?"

"Who the hell are *you*?" Lila asked. "And why are you swearing and screaming over the telephone at my friend?"

"Get off. Put Donna on again. She's the one I have to talk to."

"No," Lila said. "If you want to talk, talk to me."

"What? No. *Get off the phone.* What I have to say, it's private, and I've got to say it to her."

"That's where you're dead wrong," she said. "Say it to me. Say it to me and see if you can be angry."

"To hell with you."

"Think about it."

"You don't sound the same as her. It's her I have to talk to."

"I'm all you're going to get."

"How can I . . . I can't be . . . what *is* this stunt? Okay, listen, you have to pass something on to her."

"I don't have to do anything. Say what you're going to say."

He waited a long time, then said, "I've had thoughts."

"I'll bet you have."

"She humiliated me."

"Yes."

"I feel like Mr. Shit. Nobody talks about this. They don't show feelings like mine on television, and they aren't going to."

"No."

"They show weird people on television, men that do violent

things, stuff I won't describe. It's no problem for them. But this? No."

Lila waited.

"I feel like I'm turning into one of those plastic people on television, one of those people who's always saying crap you'd never say if you lived to be a hundred and two. I'm trying to resist it. She's trying to turn me into a loser, but I won't let her. You know what I'm doing?"

"No," Lila said. "What are you doing?"

"I'm doing something for her *that they've never done on television*. I'm working on it day and night. When I'm finished, she'll reconsider. You'll see."

"What is it?"

"It's a secret," he said bitterly. "It's not done yet."

"Maybe you should calm down," Lila told him. "Check things over. You know what they say about other fish in the sea."

"I know damn well everything they say." He sneezed. "It's hard to live. I think about her every minute. I can't work."

"Stop thinking about her."

He exhaled. "You're dumb, whoever you are. It's not the same with you women. You don't go nuts like this. Never. You don't seize up."

"Women aren't so different," she said.

"Oh no? Don't kid yourself. They're damn well different, and I'm talking in every respect. You women haven't got a thing in common with us. Not a blessed thing."

Then he clicked off. Lila agreed to stay with Donna for a couple of weeks.

At the office Donna opened an envelope addressed to her, but with no name on it. Inside was a Hallmark valentine carefully scissored into tiny asymmetrical shapes, trapezoids with handles, like jigsaw pieces. Donna turned the envelope upside down and let its contents flutter down into the wastebasket.

Later that week, on Thursday, while she was making scalloped potatoes in the kitchen, Donna heard a knock at the apartment door. A familiar sound: he was hitting the door with the heel of his fist, heavy commanding blows. Donna motioned to Lila, and Lila went over to the peephole to see who it was.

"It must be him," Lila said, her face pressed to the door. "It's a salesman's face. He's carrying something." She turned to smile at Donna. "He's so harmless-looking!" she said in a whisper. Bobby tried another knock. "Donna's not home," Lila shouted.

"Let me in," he said. "I've got something for her."

"How'd you get past the front door?" Lila asked.

"I have a key to the building. I want to talk to Donna. I have . . . I want to give her something. Who are you?"

"She's not here, and if she were, you couldn't talk to her."

"Please."

"No."

"I have this thing for her." Through the tiny convex wide-angle lens of the peephole, his face appeared smashed and flattened, as if it consisted entirely of nose. "Something I made," he said.

"I'll give it to her," Lila said, "but I will *not* open the door until you leave."

He waited. "I don't like orders. But all right. Tell her to call me. No, *I'll* call. This'll change her mind. This'll be a first in her life."

He walked off, out of sight. Whatever he had brought was somewhere below, where it couldn't be seen from inside. Donna called upstairs to ask the Seaforths to check out the hallways to make sure he wasn't hiding in the furnace closets. In two minutes Mrs. Seaforth stood outside Donna's door and said, "It's all clear. I don't see him."

Donna and Lila unlocked the door. The three women looked down at the flat package wrapped in brown paper and thick jute twine leaning against the wall. Lila bent down and brought it inside. "It's heavy," she said.

"It's not dangerous?" Mrs. Seaforth asked.

"Don't think so," Donna said. "That's not quite his style."

Lila scurried off to get a pair of scissors. Donna stood near the door, her hand up at her forehead, staring at the package and breathing unsteadily. "I haven't felt this crazy," she said, "since I learned to swim."

"What a singular man," Mrs. Seaforth said.

"Believe me, he wasn't always that way. Just at the end, when I said I didn't want to live with him. It shut down his circuits."

Lila was bending over the package, cutting the twine and tearing away the brown paper from Bobby's gift. "What sticks in my craw," she said, "is tricky packaging." She had reached another layer, a thick padding this time, of newspaper.

"Uh oh," Donna said.

"What?" Lila was pulling the tape off the folded newspaper.

"Jesus," Donna said. "It's rectangular, isn't it?"

"So?" Holding the thing at the top, with a sideways motion of her right hand, Lila pulled the newspaper away.

Inside a frame of stained oak was a composite of colored glass, twelve inches across and twenty inches down, a portrait of Donna, naked from the waist up. Drawn on a piece of yellow-gold glass, her face, though a cartoon, resembled her, except that in Bobby's drawing she was smiling enigmatically, a church-window smile, a sphinx. He had used the same yellow glass for her torso and had drawn her arms so that they hung down straight at her sides, useless, where they highlighted the drawing's presentation of her breasts, which had single dots for the nipples. Her body was surrounded by an aureole of blue, rust, and green flecks of thick glass set between the soldered strips of lead.

"Oh my my my my," Mrs. Seaforth said. "Gracious."

The reading lamp on its stalk next to the chair cast a light on the glass and through it, so that Donna saw Bobby's drawing of her body projected indistinctly on the floor, yellow running together with rust on the carpet, like an unfocused magic lantern slide.

"I hadn't thought," Donna said, but didn't finish the sentence.

"I hadn't thought," she repeated. "But who would?"

When Mrs. Seaforth had returned to her apartment upstairs, Donna and Lila sat in the living room. Lila had put some music on the phonograph to calm them.

"Maybe I should move," Donna said. "Maybe I should leave the city." She was still staring at the picture.

"No," Lila said. "Are you crazy? You can't let him do that. What's to say he wouldn't follow you? No. Absolutely not."

"Do you think he'll give up?"

"He will. Once men do you in stained glass," Lila said, "they usually quit. It's typically the last shot."

The phone rang. Lila answered it.

"I'm in a phone booth," Bobby said. "Well. Did she like it?"

"No."

"What'd she do with it?"

"They took it away. She didn't do anything with it."

"Who?"

"Why, *they* did. What difference does it make?" She looked over at Donna and saw her staring fixedly at her portrait in stained glass. More loudly, Lila said, "They took that thing out and they threw it into the trash and it broke into pieces and that's it. Nothing left but little pieces of broken glass. Nothing."

All at once Donna stood up. "Don't say that!" she said, looking at the portrait but speaking to Lila. "Don't say those things to him. Maybe he does love me. I mean, look at the picture. I don't even look like that and he's made me beautiful. Lila, I give off light in his mind!"

"I can hear her," Bobby said. "I can hear her talking to you in the room. Let me talk to her. *Put her on.*"

"No," Lila said.

"Does he want to talk to me?" Donna asked. "I bet he does. Here." She held her hand out. "Let me speak to him. Give me the phone."

"No," Lila said.

"She wants to talk to me," Bobby said. "I know she does. I can hear her."

"Bobby!" Donna said. "We didn't break it. Lila is kidding."

"What's this?" Bobby said. "I heard her say you didn't break it. Put her on. Put her on!"

"Be quiet, both of you," Lila said. "Stop this." She placed her hand over the phone's mouthpiece. "What's the matter with you?" she asked Donna.

But by this time both Donna and Bobby were talking so fast to Lila that they couldn't hear anything she said in return.

Winter Journey

✦

for Halvard Johnson

Harrelson, perpetual Ph.D. student, poverty-stricken dissertation nonfinisher, academic man of all work, gourmand, stands in the tiny kitchen cluttered with yellow note pads, a basketball, books, misplaced bookmarks, and boxes of ant killer, staring down at a dented saucepan of cold soup. Harrelson has turned on the burner, but the soup stays cold. At first he thinks that the electric company has at last made good its promise and turned off the power, yet the bare ceiling bulb continues to shower glare all over everything. The stove is not working. Harrelson grabs the stove on both sides, shaking it, creating lumpy waves in the saucepan. Harrelson's dissertation on the problem of dating Fulke Greville's poetry has not been going well. He has been sipping cheap bourbon all evening. Now, at five minutes past one o'clock, with hunger seizing him and the melancholy of his apartment inflating like a face painted on the side of a balloon, he has opened the can of soup for what his mother used to call "proper nutrition." He lifts the pan, puts his hand over the burner, feels no heat, and transfers the pan to the other burner, twisting the dial to high. He looks out the window. It is snowing a perpetual February snow. Harrelson sees the snow symbolically. Somehow it represents his refusal to sell out. Alone in the kitchen, he says to himself, "Hip hip, hooray." He likes to cheer for himself. It is something he has taught himself to do, in secret.

Turning his attention back to the soup, Harrelson notes that it is boiling. As it does, he gazes at the creation of bubbles at the surface of the soup and listens to the liquid hissing on the side of the pan. How long should soup boil before it is ready to eat? He takes the Campbell's soup can back out of the trash bag, staining his shirt sleeves with catsup as he does so, and reads the directions: DO NOT BOIL. Harrelson turns the heat off, watches the snow fall for a minute, then reaches for a bile green plastic bowl in the sink. He washes most of the corn-flakes out of the bowl and then pours in the soup. Cream of celery, his favorite. As the steam rises, he searches for a clean spoon and at last finds one with Mickey Mouse on the handle, a twenty-year-old souvenir of Disneyland.

Harrelson takes the spoon and the bowl into the living room and sits down at a wobbly desk five feet in front of the television set. In order to make room for the soup, he pushes three books to the side, and by accident one of them falls off the edge of the desk. It is an old book, a critical commentary. When it hits the floor, its binding breaks and several book-marks fall out of it. The TV set picks up only one station, which is now showing a Charlie Chan movie, *Charlie Chan at the Olympics*, starring Harrelson's favorite Chan, Sidney Toler. Fascinated, Harrelson watches as a world-class track star is discovered to have been murdered. Harrelson drinks the soup and helps himself to the bourbon. Gradually it occurs to him that the phone is ringing. Answering the phone means missing an important clue, but he rises with his eyes still on the television set and backs down the hallway into the bedroom, where the telephone sits inside the bottom drawer of his dresser to minimize the noise of its ringing whenever he has overslept.

He takes the phone out of the drawer and says hello. For a moment he hears nothing and suspects that some sort of prank is being played on him. His friends used to do such things until they found jobs and became respectable. At last a voice rises out of the static clutter and says, "I'm not asking for a favor. I'm demanding it."

"Who is this?" Harrelson asks. He knows that it is a woman's voice and that there is a slight edge of irritation to it.

"This is Meredith," the voice says. She waits. "Meredith. Your fiancée."

"Meredith!" he says delightedly. "It's been a long time. Weeks. I can't remember the last time you called over here. It's great to hear from you! Are we still engaged? What've you been up to, anyway?"

"Cut it out," she says.

"All right." There is a gunshot on the soundtrack of the movie. Harrelson's foot itches.

"I called because I need help."

"Name it," Harrelson says.

"I'm over here at the Mobil station on Stadium Avenue. My car won't run. Something about the radiator or antifreeze or the water pump. They don't make much sense here. Anyway, I need a ride home."

"I'm drunk," he says.

"How drunk?"

"How drunk what?"

"I mean, how drunk are you?"

"I don't know." He stands up in the bedroom, holding on to the telephone. "I was just having some soup when you called. Celery soup. And there's a Charlie Chan movie on. Something about death and athletics."

"What does that have to do with anything?" Harrelson can hear a cash register clacking in the background of the filling station Meredith is calling from. "Listen," she says. "I'll call a cab, except I didn't bring enough money."

"I will come," Harrelson says.

"Don't come if you're too drunk," Meredith says. "Can you stand?"

"Yes, I can stand. And," he adds, "I can sit."

"Jesus. You *are* drunk. How soon can you be here?"

"The Mobil station?" He thinks. He cannot remember where it is. He makes a guess. "Fifteen minutes."

"Are you sure?"

"It is hard to be sure," Harrelson says, "of anything in this life."

"If you come to get me, promise you won't say anything like that again. Promise?"

"Yes. I promise."

"Now listen," she says. "It's snowing out. You're not sober. You're going to have to be careful. Put on your seat belt. Avoid other cars."

"Okay, okay. Don't worry about me. I'll be there in no time." For some reason he repeats the words, "No time," before he hangs up.

He remembers to turn off the range and the television set and the lights, but he forgets to put on overshoes and gloves. When he is walking down the front steps, his feet rush out from under him, and he falls on the middle step. He is unhurt. His hands are in the snow, and when he lifts them up, he is pleased to see an outline of his hands on the step. He can feel the snow falling on his hair. He sticks his tongue out. Snow lands on his tongue's tip like airborne pieces of candy. Now he looks out at the street and sees his car, an ancient Buick, covered with snow, and snow falling in a peaceful rush underneath the streetlight, and more snow accumulating in the street, as if Meredith had thought this through and had wanted a few more difficulties than were absolutely necessary to test his loyalty. Harrelson feels a small quantity of snow working its way into his shoes. "Mr. Nice Guy," he says, still sitting on the step. He puts his hands down in the snow next to the handprints he has already made. He would like to make a snow angel in the front yard, but Meredith is waiting. He stands up, holding on to the buttons of his coat, and walks with great precision and daring to his car.

As he tries to find his car keys, scattered in his pocket, he holds his head up and looks with an expression of vague speculation at his car and the street. There is certainly a great deal of snow all over everything. Some sort of muffled siren howls gently in the distance. Up the street an unclearly outlined figure is shoveling his sidewalk. Harrelson thinks of Meredith waiting for him in the sinister gas station and renews his efforts to find his car keys. He grasps a number of keys, pulls them out, and watches with neutralized dismay as several of them plop into the snow, leaving slots behind that, Charlie Chan—like, Harrelson uses for pursuit and detection. With all the cold, snowy keys gathered up in his hands, he selects the one that unlocks the car door, deposits the rest in his pocket, and gets in.

He says a prayer, turns the key in the ignition, and the engine starts after a few cranks. As it warms up, exhaust fumes begin seeping up from the floor. Harrelson reaches for a fugitive cigarette on the dashboard, left there by some random hitchhiker—he adores hitchhikers and picks them up at every opportunity—and lights up before getting out to clear the windshield. With his bare hands he sweeps the front and side windows, leaving a bit of ice on the glass for the defroster to take care of. When he is back inside the car, he looks in the rearview mirror and observes that he has not cleared the back window. He shrugs to himself and inhales from the cigarette, which brings on a fit of coughing. He opens the window, looks out into the street to see if anything is coming, prays to his guardian angel, puts the car into gear, and steps on the gas.

In any university town there are hundreds of men like Harrelson, out late at night buying pizzas, sitting at bars sipping their beers quietly, or roaming the streets in their old clunkers. They are all afraid of going home, afraid of looking again at the sheets of clean typewriter paper and the notebooks bare of written thought. They are afraid of facing again their sullen wives and lovers, their tattered and noisy children, if they have any. Against the odds, they refuse to succeed, and the wives and lovers know this and understand it as a rebuke to themselves and family life.

"You won't grow up" is Meredith's succinct way of putting

it. She has put it to him this way many times, most recently two months ago, in December, the last time they talked. They were sitting in her apartment, its cleanliness a stark contrast to Harrelson's squalor. Meredith is an accountant, a serious worker with a serious income. They have known each other since high school, when their romance took shape. This romance is now, according to Meredith, on its frail last legs. The fireplace in Meredith's apartment supplied potent warmth against the December cold, and she had put out the brandy, a V.S.O.P. Despite the appearances, however, the evening was tense, the screws of pressure twisted by Meredith's contempt for her four-year fiancé. "Look at you," Meredith said. "Look at what you've done with your life. You could have been brilliant. I feel so sorry for you. I don't want to marry a man I feel sorry for."

"I agree with you," Harrelson said. "Pity is a bad foundation for any marriage."

"Honey," she said, "I don't want to break off with you, because I do love you, but I've got other things going for me, and I can't hold them off forever. You know I've been going out with other men."

Harrelson nodded. He was silently praying that she wouldn't continue in this vein.

"And many of them," Meredith continued, "are very nice: very bright, successful, and, uh, you know, handsome. I can't wait forever."

Harrelson thought she had said everything possible to wound him. So he said, "I've made real progress this month. Really, I have. I'm only about fifty pages away from finishing." He smiled. "Fifty pages away from the degree and a good job."

"You're thirty years old," she said. "You're getting too old to hire."

"Oh no." This exclamation from Harrelson was more an outcry than a denial.

Meredith leaned forward. Her eyes were glittering.

"Honey," she said, "it's just that I don't want to be married to a nerd."

This was more than even Harrelson could take. He put down his brandy, got into his coat, and left. Because he was Harrelson and because he lived according to a consistent style, he did not shout at her or make an accusation in return. He thought his guardian angels were on vacation and had failed to muzzle Meredith. They allowed her to say what shouldn't have been said. What no one else knows is that although he attends no church, Harrelson is in an almost constant state of prayer. He has familiars in the spirit world.

The inside of his car smells of burned electrical wire and popcorn. As he exhales smoke from the hitchhiker's leftover cigarette, a fog appears and frosts visibly on the inside windshield in a pattern of continuous webbing. The car pulls out of its parking spot, its engine making tappet noises that rise to a whine as the back wheels spin on the ice. Fishtailing, the car skids down the street. Harrelson has no snow tires; in fact, the tires are bald. He plans his route in an effort to avoid hills and valleys. Within a minute he has forgotten the route he has planned.

Despite the snow and the streetlights, the street is darker than it should be: a stygian street. Harrelson remembers that one of his headlights has blown out. His hands, gloveless, are aching, numb. And he feels ready to doze off, despite the cold. His drunkenness communicates itself to him as a fanatic desire to crawl into bed and pull the blankets up. He is seeing two of everything: two sets of streetlights, two streets, two steering wheels, two dashboards. And two red lights, both of which he now runs, unable and unwilling to stop the car before entering the intersection. With scholarly interest he observes that he has missed hitting a red Dodge Aries by perhaps two or three feet. For the first time he understands that it might be a moral offense against God and man to be out driving in a snowstorm, drunk. But it is more of an offense before women to be a nerd, a coward, a man *who will not help*. He accelerates.

At high speed, in snow, the houses fan by him on either side, visually glazed and impacted into smears of windows, doors, roofs, unremoved Christmas lights, chimneys, and, again and again, interior lights, the lights of domesticity left on late at night to ward off prowlers and intruders. Where is the street? It has not been plowed. He continues driving. Continuous motion is important. A dog rushes out in front of the car. It is about the size of an enlarged rat and has a narrow snout. It stops in a seizure of panic. Harrelson hears no thump and feels no impact. He opens his window and looks out into the street receding behind him. The dog stands motionless, watching Harrelson's car as Harrelson watches the dog, tire tracks imprinted on either side of it in the snow.

"Run over," Harrelson says aloud, "but not run down." He laughs to himself, feels the need again to doze off as the heater gradually warms up the car, but resists. He decides to recite poetry. "'Fie, fond desire,'" he quotes from Fulke Greville, "'"think you that love wants glory/Because your shadows do yourself benight?/The hopes and fears of lust may make men sorry,/But love still in herself finds her delight.'" Harrelson hits a parked car. He knows he has hit it from the sound and the impact, but he hasn't seen it because the windows on the right side are coated with snow. After hitting the car, Harrelson's Buick bounces back into the middle of the street and begins to skid toward the other side. It hits another parked car, slides for twenty feet, then stops. Glass and plastic have been heard, breaking. He puts the car into first gear and continues down the street, which now looks darker than ever. "Uh oh," he says aloud. "I smashed the other headlight."

I'm not funny, I'm a risk, he thinks.

Other cars are around him; some are moving, others are not. The ones that *are* moving honk at him and blink their lights. "I am a hazard to myself," Harrelson says, passing a large building, lit up on each floor, as if people are still working. He thinks he sees someone on the third floor looking down at him, an expression of pity on the stranger's face. The thought of a stranger's pity makes Harrelson's eyes smart. Studying the dashboard, trying not to cry, Harrelson steps on the gas, hurrying down the street toward an area where the overhead lights are not so apparent. Sudden darkness: the car plunges into it. He passes two garages and a butcher shop with sausages hanging in the window, the glass lightly covered with snow. What if I hit a child, he thinks. What if I do that.

Now, having made a circle, Harrelson is back under lights in the business district, his car out of control, advancing down the street sideways. He grabs the seat, ready for a collision, and feels the foam under his hand. In front of him is a department-store window, moving from right to left, in which a bald dummy sits wearing a blue polyester leisure suit. He turns the wheel in the direction of the skid, and the Buick straightens out. He feels a sudden elation. He *can* control himself, the car, the weather conditions. He slows down, steers the car toward the curb, and shuts off the engine. He is drowsy. He will take a brief nap. He bends his head down on his chest and within thirty seconds falls asleep. Instantly a dream starts up. In the dream he is driving the car through a blizzard on his way to get Meredith. The car skids, hits a tree, and there is a bright flash. But he continues driving, reaches her apartment, gets out, and enters the building. He ascends the stairs and walks into her living room. Her back is to him as she works at the stove. "I'm here," he says. "Hi," she says, turning around. But now she cannot see him. "Honey," she says, "is that you?" Her eyes scan the room. "Where are you?" Her voice rises. "I can't see you."

He wakes up, full of the intuition that his life is a disaster. He is the sort of person other people cite in order to feel that they themselves are well off: they could live the way Harrelson does. They could *be* Harrelson. They could think Harrelson's grubby thoughts. He starts the car. Then, a non-Catholic, he makes the sign of the cross. He has not been arrested. His guardian angel is in the car with him, working overtime. Once in a dream the angel identified himself as Matthew and told Harrelson that he, Harrelson, was under his, Matthew's, protection. Since that dream, Harrelson has been lazier, more slipshod; sometimes he thinks the dream may have been his undoing.

He drives and drives. He is lost. Visibility is poor. He sees no landmarks. He looks at his watch: he has been in the car for twenty minutes. The windshield wipers move slowly, heavily, like Harrelson's eyes.

And just at the moment when Harrelson thinks that he is K. and will never reach the Mobil station no matter how long or how hard he tries, there it is. First it appears through the curtain of snow as a glowing patch of light without any solid outlines. Then, second by second, he sees the snowy spotlights, the fluorescent lights over the gas pumps, the aquamarine station itself with its closed garage doors, and now he sees a small old man in a black overcoat filling his car with gas at the self-service pump, and now, closer, he sees an attendant gazing in his direction with something like stupefaction, at Harrelson behind the wheel, in his dark car with no headlights.

The attendant walks over to him. Harrelson's head is bowed and he is muttering. Though the attendant doesn't know it, Harrelson is thanking his familiars, making concrete spiritual promises. The man, who is covered with snow, knocks on the window. Harrelson looks at him and rolls it down.

"You okay, buddy?" the man asks. He is wearing a blue parka and gazes in at Harrelson with friendly curiosity. His mouth is open, and Harrelson can see the huge gap of his mouth and his bad, crisscrossed teeth.

"Yeah, I'm all right."

"Reason I asked is, you got no headlights."

"I know." Harrelson suddenly remembers. "Is there a woman waiting inside the station? She's waiting for me."

"Yeah," the man says, "she's here. What happened to your face, buddy?"

"My face is all right." He looks toward the door and sees Meredith coming out, all smiles, dressed in her warm red winter coat, her brown boots, and black gloves. Harrelson tries to take his hands off the wheel and finds that he is having difficulty uncurling his fingers. Meredith crosses the front of the car and opens the door on the passenger's side.

"You should put new headlights in," the man says, but now Harrelson is closing the window.

He turns toward Meredith, who, instead of smiling, looks horror-struck. "John," she says, "honey, what happened to you?"

He turns to her, his eyes full of gratitude. "Well," he says, "I drove over here."

"No," she says, "I mean this." She takes off her right glove and raises her hand to his face. When she touches his skin, he feels a dull burning on his left cheek. "There's a cut here. A gash. It's been bleeding. What'd you do?"

"I have no idea."

"Did you have an accident coming over here?"

"Two." He holds up two fingers. "I had *two* accidents."

"You must have hit your head against the window or the . . . this." She reaches over and touches the latch for opening the no-draft window. "You may need stitches."

"No," he says. "It doesn't hurt." He smiles. "It's good to see you." Now he feels happy. "I made it! I made it over here!" He looks at her with a private, conspiratorial expression. "The roads were terrible, and I'm not sober."

"I know." She looks at him, top to bottom. "Get out and come over on this side," she says. "I'll drive back to my place. I don't want you driving any more."

"All right." He does as he is told. Now, with Meredith be-

hind the wheel, he sits back, and the pain in his cheek flares
up. She is driving. Harrelson does not know where they are.
He feels sleepy. She is saying something, but he is not quite
sure that it makes any sense. Then the car is parked and Meredith has helped him out, and he is sitting in her living room,
his face washed lightly with a washcloth, his cut covered with
antiseptic cream. Meredith's radio is on, and Dietrich Fischer-
Dieskau is singing.

> Habe ja doch nichts begangen
> Dass ich Menschen sollte scheu'n—
> Welch' ein törichtes Verlangen
> Treibt mich in die Wüstenei'n?

"'I've done no wrong,'" Harrelson translates, hoping to im-
press Meredith, "'to shun other men, so what is it that sends
me out into the wilderness?'"

"That's the song?"

"That's it."

"What is it?"

"I don't know. It's German."

"I know," she says. "Isn't it interesting?"

"I guess so."

"There." She is finished cleaning Harrelson's cheek. "It's a
smaller cut than I thought. Aren't you going to take off your
jacket?" He nods but does nothing. She unzips it and helps
him out of it. He is not really looking toward her but toward the
stereo radio. "Poor John," she says. "But listen: thanks for
getting me."

"You're welcome."

"I didn't realize how drunk you were."

He waves his hand. "That's all right."

"Are you cold?" He nods. "Come in and take a warm bath."
She leads him into the bathroom and sits him down while she

fills the tub. The warmth in the bathroom makes him sleepy again. He feels her taking his clothes off and helping him into the bathwater. The water's heat is intensely painful on his chilled feet, like icepicks thrust into the skin. She is still talking. He is bent over in the water, looking at the hair on his legs. "I've made a decision," she is saying. "I'm not going to marry you."

Harrelson nods. "I know."

"How did you know? I've only just decided."

"I just knew." He does not look at her.

"I decided a few days ago. I'm sorry."

"It's all right." He puts his hand on the surface of the bathtub water and moves it back and forth, creating waves.

"I need more security than you can give me," she says. "I'm sorry, but that's the way it is."

"Of course." Now he turns his head toward her. "Please don't say any more."

"I won't."

"Thank you." He takes the soap and washes his arms and chest. "You know, I don't feel very good."

"Where?" she asks. "Is it your face?"

He shakes his head. "I don't feel very good anywhere."

She stands up and turns away. She opens the medicine cabinet and examines the bottles. "Want some aspirin?"

"No."

He rises to his feet unsteadily in the tub. Meredith turns around, then takes his hand. With her other hand she reaches for a towel and dries him off. "You need some sleep," she says. "We both need some sleep." They walk together toward the bedroom, and Harrelson slips between the cold sheets. He hears the radio being turned off. In a moment, Meredith is in her nightgown, next to him. "We can still be friends," she says.

"Yes."

She leans over toward him and kisses him lightly. "We can

still make love. There's no harm in that." His eyes are closed, but he nods. "Do you want to?"

"No," he whispers. "I don't."

"Maybe next time," she says. "When you haven't had so much to drink." He nods, then reaches his arms around her and rests his hands in their accustomed place below her breasts. As he falls asleep, Harrelson realizes that, after all, they *are* friends. Meredith does not think he will ever be a husband. Probably she is right. He does not have it in him to take care of another human being. It will never happen. As he drifts over, Harrelson has a premonition that he may not live for long. With what resistance he has left, he dismisses the idea as weakness, a bout of self-pity.

As soon as he is asleep, he finds himself in the company of his familiars. The faces that surround him are illuminated from within, and what they say is articulated in the language of angel speech. One of them welcomes him by saying, "What two time fine," and another replies with "And certainly certainly more sunsets provided than last February." These angels have no interest whatever in meaning. They say whatever pops into their heads. But it hardly matters because they gather around him, all smiles, and are pleased to be in his company. Some dispense with words and speak in music. Archaic joy washes over him. One angel detaches himself from the rest and says, "John, you are quite a poor sort," and it is meant as a compliment. Harrelson accepts the compliment. He feels another one of them bend down and kiss him lightly on the head. He is being gathered up.

But no: at once there is a point on the horizon, a point insistent with earthly magnetism, drawing Harrelson away toward the world, the real world that made Plato so unhappy, and he wakes up, hungover, in Meredith's arms, the sun rising orange over a field of snow. It is daytime, and Meredith is kissing him, and telling him he must go home now.

Saul and Patsy
Are Getting Comfortable
in Michigan

✦

Some time after they had rented the farmhouse with loose brown aluminum siding on Whitefeather Road, Saul began glaring out the west window after dinner, as if he were angry at the flat uncultivated farmland for being farmland instead of glass and cement. "No sane Jew," he said, "ever lived on a dirt road." Patsy reminded him of Poland, Russia, and the nineteenth century. Then she pointed down at the Scrabble board and told him to play. To spite her, he spelled out "axiom" over a triple-word score, for forty-two points. "That was different, pal," Saul said, after another measured minute, shaking his head. "That was when everyone but the landowners lived on dirt roads. It was a democracy of dirt roads." Patsy was clutching her Hires root beer with one hand and arranging the letters on her slate with the other. Her legs were crossed in the chair, and the root-beer bottle was positioned against the instep of her bare right foot. She looked up at him and smiled. He couldn't help it; he smiled back.

"I forgot to tell you," she said. "There's a mouse in the trap downstairs."

"Is it dead?" He gave her an unsprung look.

"It looks real dead. You know—smashed back, slightly open mouth, and the usual eyes. Oh, they're dead eyes, Saul, I'm telling you. Joan Crawford eyes. I'll spare you the description. You'll see the whole scene soon enough."

"I did the dishes," Saul whined.

"*I* can throw the mouse out," Patsy said, leaning back, taking a swig of the root beer. "But it'll cost you plenty. Emotionally and sexually. You do it, and there might be something in it for you."

"What?"

"The power negotiator," she said, "doesn't show her hand too soon."

He stood up, shaking the letters on the board, and clomped in his white socks to the kitchen, where the flashlight was stuck to the refrigerator with a magnet that was so weak that the flashlight kept sliding down to the floor. "I didn't say you had to do it now," Patsy shouted. "You could wait until the game is over."

"I can't concentrate," Saul said, flicking the flashlight off and on, "thinking about the corpse of that mouse." The batteries were low; the light from the bulb was brown. He opened the door to the basement, fanning stale air, and stared down the steps into the darkness that smelled of must and heating oil. He didn't like the basement; at night, in bed, he thought he heard crying from down there. "You'll do anything to beat me at Scrabble," Saul shouted. "This is gamesmanship, honey. Don't tell me otherwise." He snapped on the wall switch, and the shadows of the steps sawtoothed themselves in front of him. "I *really* don't like this," he said, walking down the stairs, a sliver from the banister leaping into the heel of his palm. "This is not my idea of a good time." He heard Patsy say something, consoling and inaudible.

On his left were the wooden shelves once meant for storing preserves. On these shelves mason jars, empty and gathering dust, were now lined up unevenly. Saul and Patsy's landlord, Mr. Munger, a retired farmer and preacher, had thrown their lids together into a heap on a lower shelf. The washtubs were on Saul's right, and in front of him, four feet away, was the mouse. The mouse had been flattened by the trap, and its tiny yellow incisors were showing at the sides of its mouth.

Saul grunted, loosened the trap, and picked up the mouse by the tail, which felt like cold rubber. His fingers brushed against the animal's downy fur, soft as milkweed pods. With his other hand he held the flashlight. He heard other mice scratching in the darkened basement corners. After climbing the stairs and opening the back door, he set the flashlight down: the cold air and the darkness made his flesh prickle. Still holding the mouse, he took four steps into the backyard. Feeling a scant moment of pity, he threw the mouse toward the field, its body arcing over the tiny figure of a radio transmitting tower, one pulsing red light at its tip, on the horizon. Saul breathed in the cold air. The desolation of the landscape excited him. He felt the snow through his socks.

He walked into the living room, where Patsy was wrapped in a blanket. "Good news and bad news," Saul said. "The good news is that I threw the mouse out. The bad news is that it, she, was pregnant. Maybe that's good news. You decide. By the way, I see that you've wrapped yourself in a blanket. Now why is that? Too cold in here?"

She had dimmed the light, turning the three-way bulb to its low wattage. She wasn't sitting in the chair; she was lying on the sofa, the root beer nowhere in sight. With a grand gesture she parted the blanket: she had taken off her clothes except for the panties, and just above her breasts she had placed six Scrabble letters:

H I
S A U L

"Nine points," he said, settling himself down next to her, breathing in her odor, a clean celerylike smell. He picked the letters off her skin with his teeth and one by one gently spat them down onto the rug.

"I guess it's good news," Patsy said, "that we don't have all those baby mice in a mouse nursery down there." She kissed him.

"Umm," Saul said. "This was what was in it for me?"

"Plain old married love," Patsy said, helping him take his jeans off. Then she lifted up her pelvis as he removed her panties. "Plain old married love is only what it is."

He moved down again next to her as she unbuttoned his shirt. He said, "Sometimes I think you'll go to any length to avoid losing in Scrabble. I think it's a character weakness on your part. Neurotic rigidity. David Shapiro talks about this in his book on neurotic styles. Check it out. It's a loser's trick. I spelled out 'axiom' and you saw the end of your possibilities."

"It's not a trick," she said, absentmindedly stroking his thighs and penis, while he pointed his index finger and pretended to write with it across her breasts and then down across her abdomen. "Hey," she said, "what're you writing with that finger?"

"'I love Patsy,'" he said. "I'm not writing it, I'm *printing* it."

"Why?"

"Make it more readable."

"'I love Patsy,'" she said. "Seventeen points."

"Sixteen."

"A V is worth four." His eyes were closed; with one hand he was kneading her right breast, and with the other he wrote other words with imaginative lettering across her hips. "I don't remember making love in this room before. Especially not with the shades up." She stretched to kiss his face and to tease her tongue briefly into his mouth. Then she trailed her finger across his back. "I can do that, too." She traced the letters with her finger just under his shoulders.

"That was an I," Saul said.

"Yes."

"'I love Saul'?" he asked. "Is that what you're writing?"

"You're so conceited. So self-centered."

"The curtains are parted," he said. "The neighbors will see."

"We don't have neighbors. This is the rural middle of American nowhere. Always has been."

"People will drive by on Whitefeather Road and see us fucking happily on the sofa." He waited. "They might be shocked."

"We're married," she said. "We've been married for three years."

"Ah, you're a wicked woman, Patsy."

"You keep quoting Bette Davis movies," she said, sliding her hands up the sides of his chest. "That's a habit you should swear off. Let those people watch us. They might learn something." She slithered down to kiss the scar on his knee, then moved up. "The only thing I mind about sex," she said after another minute, "and I've said this before, is that it cuts down on the small talk."

"We talk a lot," Saul said, positioning himself next to her, and finally entering her. He grunted, then said, "I think we talk more than most people. No, I'm sure of it. We've always jabbered. Most people don't talk this much, men especially." He was making genial moves inside her. "Of course it's hard to tell. I mean, who does surveys?"

"Oh, Saul," she said. "You know, I'm glad I know you. Out here, in the wilds, a girl needs a pal, she really does. You're my pal, Saul. You are."

"It's true," he said. "We're buddies. Bosom buddies." He kissed a breast. On an impulse, he twisted slightly so that he could reach over to the card table behind him and scoop up a handful of Scrabble letters from the playing board.

"What're you doing?" she asked.

"I'm going to baptize you," he said, slowly dropping the tiled letters on her face and shoulders and breasts.

"God," she said, as a P and an E fell into her hair, "to think I wanted to distract you with a mouse caught in a trap."

Saul had been hired in June of the previous summer to teach American history, journalism, and speech in the Five Oaks High School. Five Oaks was not what he and Patsy had had in mind; they had planned to settle down in Boston, or, in the worst-case scenario, the north side of Chicago. They'd been working at office jobs in Evanston at the time, and one day, driving home, Saul began to shout about the supervision and the surveillance, how he couldn't breathe or open his office window. "Budget projections for a bus company," he said, "is no longer meaningful work." He rambled on about being recertified for secondary school because he needed to contribute to what he called "the great project of undoing the dumbness that's been done."

"Saul," Patsy said, sitting on the passenger side and working at a week-old Sunday *Times* crossword, "you're underlining your words again."

"This country is falling into the hands of the rich and stupid," Saul grumbled, waving his right hand in an all-purpose gesture at the windshield. "It's getting worse and worse. The conspiracy of the inane starts in the schools, but it gets big results in business. Everywhere I've looked lately I've seen a genial stupid person in a position of tremendous responsibility. We're being undermined by oafs and dolts. This has got to stop."

"There's *lots* of stupidity out there, Saul," Patsy said, glancing up at a stoplight. "A big supply. You think you're going to clear it away?" She waited. "The light just turned green. Pay attention to the road, please." She smiled. "'"Drive," he said.'"

"I'm the big man for the job," Saul said. "This country needs me."

"Well of course." She scratched her hair. "Nine letters for 'acidic.' First letter is V and the fourth one is R."

"'Vitriolic,'" Saul said. "And you could get recertified, too. Or you could insinuate yourself into a bureaucracy and rancorously reorganize it. Boston is full of dumb low-IQ deadwood. God knows you can clear out deadwood. It's been proved."

"Finger-exercise composer," Patsy said. "Six letters, last letter Y and first letter C."

"Czerny."

"Boston, huh?" She gazed at the sky. "It's sort of hard to get teaching jobs there, isn't it?"

After Saul was hired in Five Oaks, Michigan, in June, he found a ladder in his landlord's shed that was long enough to get him up to the roof of the house on Whitefeather Road. He'd been exploring Mr. Munger's shed while Patsy was at the IGA getting the groceries, and when she returned, he was sitting on the south peak with his legs dangling over the edge. Patsy put the grocery bags down on the driveway. "I won't scream," she said. "But I do have questions."

"Good," he said.

"Saul. Be truthful. Why are you sitting on the roof of our house?"

"Thinking," he shouted. "Looking at the horizon." He smiled down at her. "At the view."

"There's no view," she said. "Nothing to see."

"I was hoping. I thought maybe I'd see something. A hill, maybe."

"No hills, honey. Remember? We agreed. No hills. Just drainage ditches. Come down from the roof, Saul, before you fall and kill yourself."

"Patsy," he shouted. "How'd we end up here?"

"Times were hard," she said, quoting the Wizard of Oz, "so we took the job." She watched him. "Remember? It was the stupid crusade. *Against* stupidity, I mean."

"Oh, right. Look at this," he said despairingly, pointing at the land around their home. "You know, pal, I think we made a terrible mistake. All I see up here is dirt roads and farmers sitting on their front porches reading *The Protocols of the Elders of Zion.*"

"Saul," she said, "they watch television now. Also, it's too early for paranoia. They never saw a Jew before. Please come down. I've got to take these groceries in. Please don't break your neck."

"It's not Boston," he said, edging toward the ladder. "And it's not Chicago. It's not Des Moines. It's not even, God help us, Fargo." One of the shingles loosened and slid to the gutter. The ladder trembled as he began to make his way down. "It's scary up there, honey. It's a view for adults. Not for kids. Kids couldn't handle it." He looked straight into her eyes.

"I hope—" she said, pausing.

"—you don't go nuts out here? Me too. Me too."

Their nearest neighbor, Mrs. O'Neill, looked so much like Thelma Ritter that Saul and Patsy smirked at each other when she introduced herself at their door one Friday afternoon, peering inside as she asked them for a bottle of molasses she could borrow for cookies. As soon as Patsy found the bottle of Br'er Rabbit, Mrs. O'Neill invited them over to sample the cookies she had already made, and those she would make with their molasses. When Saul and Patsy pulled into her driveway, her garage door began to go up, even though Mrs. O'Neill had arrived before they had and her car was already inside. An iron coach-and-horse weathervane stood on an iron stalk atop the garage's cupola. Mrs. O'Neill stood near the geranium-surrounded flagpole, holding on to a pushbutton signal box, her eyes squinched.

"I'm garage-poor," she said, pressing the button again to make the door go down. "But I never could resist a toy." She laughed and touched her forehead with her hand. She offered the garage-door opener to Saul, who pressed the button. The door began to open again. "I said to myself, well, I need the gadget because I'm a single lady out here, the safety feature, but even that doesn't explain the curtains." Mrs. O'Neill's garage had windows at the front and sides, with lace curtains.

"A good garage is important," Patsy said, and immediately Saul smiled.

"That's it," Mrs. O'Neill said, picking a bug off Patsy's shoulder. "I'll tell you what it was, since you'll discover it soon enough. A project. I need a project. The sound of hammers keeps me awake. Now you, Saul, you trot inside that garage and look at that gizmo in case you want to build one yourself while Patsy and I go inside and fiddle for a couple of minutes in the kitchen."

Mrs. O'Neill grabbed Patsy's arm and pulled her toward the back door of the house.

Saul walked in a lackadaisical fashion toward Mrs. O'Neill's sheltered Buick. A steady wind from the unplowed fields to the south blew into the garage, agitating the lace curtains. The interior smelled of raw lumber and fresh paint, along with the fainter but more dense odor of overheated electrical wiring. Saul looked up as instructed at Mrs. O'Neill's new project. Unmechanical to a fault, he was unable to guess what structural-dynamic principles were involved in lifting a garage door up a set of tracks. With his head tilted back, he saw the company name on the side of the motor: GENIE. He felt suddenly dizzy. He inhaled quickly and leaned his arm against Mrs. O'Neill's car. He glanced out through the door and saw his own car, and then, beyond it, the horizon line of the Saginaw Valley, and gold-brown topsoil whipped and scattered in spirals. He sat down on the bumper and put his head in his hands.

From the house came the sound of singing: Mrs. O'Neill's voice—Patsy didn't sing—a choir-loft soprano, a thin Irish upper register, without resonance or depth, piercing as a factory whistle. Saul listened, the hair on the back of his neck slowly beginning to rise. *"Mi chiamano Mimi,"* she was singing, *"il perchè non so. Sola, mi fo il pranzo da me stesa."* She sang half the aria, the sound careening out of the house and dispersing in the yard. Saul felt his own mouth opening. A bird fluttered into the garage, changed course in an instant, and flew out, alighting at the top of Mrs. O'Neill's flagpole. Saul wanted the garage door shut. He pressed the button. When he opened the garage a minute later, Patsy was standing in front of it on the driveway, a plate of cookies in her hand.

"Aren't you funny?" she said.

"She sings." They looked at each other. "Where is she?"

"Yes, she sings. Still in the house. I noticed she had some opera records, and she said that she and her late lamented husband Earl used to listen to the Texaco broadcasts. She sings in church."

"I guessed."

"Anyway, she has all these records and she managed to learn some of the words. That was a demo she gave me. Want some of these cookies?"

"Of course. Dumb question." He reached out and grabbed four off the plate.

"She had some questions about you."

"About me?"

"That's why she wanted you to inspect her garage."

"Oh."

"She thought it was safe to ask me. Woman to woman."

"What sort of questions."

"Friendly questions."

"Such as?"

"Do Jews eat cookies?"

"Do Jews eat cookies."

"That's right. 'Does he go to a temple?' 'Does he mind living here among us?' She asked if we were rich. She asked if I was one of you." Patsy bit into a cookie and wiped the sweat off her forehead with the back of her hand.

"What'd you tell her?"

"I said I was once a Lutheran but now I was your wife."

"And what did she say?"

"She said she was so glad that you liked cookies."

"There she is."

Patsy turned around as Mrs. O'Neill leaned out of the back door to wave them both inside. "I won't sing anymore," she shouted. "You two children can come in now. It's safe."

Through the summer they visited Mrs. O'Neill every two weeks for a Sunday-afternoon picnic in the shade of her linden tree. They found Patsy a Tuesday-Thursday-Saturday job as a clerk in the Rexall Buy-Rite. They played Scrabble and Jeopardy, Trivial Pursuit and chess, and they listened to all their records at least twice. Patsy suggested that they travel north to explore Traverse City and the Upper Peninsula, but Saul complained about what he called "the Indian problem" and said travel was dangerous in those locales. When Patsy asked him what Indian problems he was talking about, he said that of course the Department of Natural Resources had kept the problem under wraps but that he, Saul, knew . . . things. She could not budge him from his irony.

With all the time they had, they made love frequently, Patsy having decided that they should try it in every room in the house. By August they had drawn themselves together in the living room, dining room, and kitchen; one afternoon late in the month they spread out a blanket in the backyard, out of sight of Whitefeather Road, and worked up what Saul called "a good erotic sweat." Patsy claimed she had never made love outdoors before and said she liked it, it was state-fairish, except for the grass on her bare back—they had crawled away from the blanket. She worried about ants, for which she had a repugnance. She said she liked looking into the sky and thought it would be neat to gaze at a cloud while having an orgasm. They waited for the perfect cloud, and then Saul watched her as she came. True to her word, she kept her eyes wide open, focused on the distance.

Saul having his hair cut: Five Oaks' barbershop contained eight chairs, a black-and-white Emerson television set on a wheeled table, six rabbit skulls (one with a bullet hole neatly penetrating the left side) superglued to the mirror above the cash register, a set of old *Esquires*, and one barber with gray hair and thick black-rimmed glasses. When Saul sat down in the chair, the barber tucked his cover cloth under Saul's collar and whistled between his teeth. "Don't see hair like yours much around here," he said. "It's almost kinky, wouldn't you say?"

Saul said it was almost kinky and what he basically wanted was a trim.

The barber set to work, sneaking looks at *General Hospital*, which appeared in a pointillist quilt of snow and interference on the Emerson. Saul closed his eyes but opened them five minutes later, feeling the barber's hand resting peacefully on his shoulder, the scissors motionless in his hair. "Say," Saul said, nudging the barber's stomach with his elbow. "Are we awake here? Hello?"

The barber inhaled, exhaled, snorted, and said, sure, of course he was awake, what made him think he was asleep? The scissors started up again, their tips scraping Saul's scalp. "Could be I did doze off there for a minute," the barber said. "But it's only the third . . . no, fourth time I've ever done that in this particular shop. I can sleep standing up, you see. Learned it in the army. Like a horse. I must've fallen asleep on account of your hair is so thick to cut. Are you from around here? We don't see hair like yours too much in this town. It's so hard to cut I believe it made me take a nap."

"We just moved here," Saul said, to explain.

"From Detroit, I'll bet," the barber said. "They see hair like yours a lot in Detroit, I hear."

Once classes at the high school had started, Saul's route took him down Whitefeather Road for two miles before he turned left onto County Road E. On County Road E he pressed the car's CruiseControl button and removed his foot from the accelerator for the six-mile straightaway. There were no curves to the road; there never had been. With his foot off the accelerator, he ate his breakfast of Patsy's Pillsbury muffins washed down with low-caffeine cola while he shaved with his Remington cordless and listened to the car's tape deck, his early-morning music friend, Thelonious Monk, whose attitude toward daylight was offhand, smart, and antirural.

Three miles down County Road E and half a mile before it intersected with Bailey-Fraser Road, was the morning's bad news, standing on two legs on an average of three days a week. This bad news wore a hat and a jacket, sported gray socks and thick glasses—on some days he looked like the barber's brother—and he stared at Saul and his car with a mean hateful expression.

The first few times Saul passed him, he waved; he didn't expect a counterwave, and he didn't get it. Standing like a sentry, the man stood glaring, an unwobbling pivot, his arms down at his sides. At last, in October, Saul slowed down on Tuesday, and on Wednesday he stopped. He leaned out and said, "You want to say hello? Here's your opportunity. The name's Saul. Howdy."

His greeting was returned with a blank look. Slowly, carefully, Saul lifted the finger to him, and then hit the accelerator.

Saul to Patsy at dinner: "There's this peckerwood ghoul standing in his yard every morning giving me the Big Stare, and he's got this porkpie hat nailed to his skull, and what I think is, he's on to me, the schmuck hates Jews. Have I mentioned him? I have? He wants me out. One of these days he's going to hoist a rifle and get me between the eyes."

"You're paranoid." They were in the dining room and had been listening to Nielsen's *Four Temperaments* Symphony.

"I've got a right to be paranoid. History encourages it. Plus, the man hates me. And for no reason: he doesn't know me. I bet he's a colonel in a Minuteman cadre. I'm going to get the JDL on his case. They'll blow him out of his yard into Lake Huron."

Patsy stood up. "I'll call Mrs. O'Neill."

"You'd better not." Saul looked alarmed. "What if she's part of this conspiracy?"

Patsy shrugged. In five minutes she was back.

"Well?" While they ate, they had also been playing Scrabble, and when she was out of the room, Saul had traded two of his bad letters for better ones.

"Mrs. O'Neill says his name is Bart Connell."

"A rabid anti-Semite."

"Not exactly. He has Alzheimer's. He lives with his daughter. They don't let him stray out of the yard. He used to wander off, onto the road. He flew bombing missions during the Second World War. Then he worked as a mechanic at Byer's Ford. Could fix anything. Now he can't, quote, figure out how to put a key to a keyhole, unquote. Shame on you, Saul. He's a plain good man with all his mind gone."

Saul sulked.

"And put those two letters back," she said. "I saw what you did."

Saul's students were younger than he remembered students were supposed to be for high school. Some were intelligent; others were not. How Saul performed in class didn't seem to make that much difference, one way or another. Those who were stupid stayed that way.

In the teachers' lounge, the talk was of their children, or health insurance, or places to go on vacation in July, or what had been on television the night before, or gossip. Sometimes Saul joined in. He often thought he was observing them and himself from a distance.

Saul woke at night, thinking that the meaning of a serious career, of adulthood generally, had escaped him. In the middle of the night, life did not seem to be the joke he once thought it might be, in college. At such times he would take Patsy, awake or asleep, into his arms. He wanted to admit that he had made a terrible mistake and that they were suffering the consequences. Sounds came up from the basement. Never again would they live in the fully human world. The trouble with Patsy was that she said she liked it fine in Five Oaks. All he could do was hold on to her and wait for the hours to pass.

He climbed to the roof of the house in the fall to correct quizzes and tests. Staring out over the fields, he felt his attention disperse into the landscape, floating gradually into the topsoil, like pollen. Then he would look down and underline a sentence fragment in green ink.

Saul's mother, Delia, a boisterous widow who swam a mile a day, played bridge on Tuesdays, tennis on Fridays, called her son every other weekend. When Patsy answered, Saul's mother talked about recipes or the weather; when Saul answered, she discussed life and the nature of fate. In February, after Saul and Patsy had been in Five Oaks for nine months, she said that she had heard from a friend that wonderful teaching jobs were opening up outside Boston, and even closer, *right here, outside Baltimore*. I heard this, she said, from Mrs. Rauscher. Saul listened to his mother go on for five minutes, and then he stopped her.

"Ma," he said. "We're staying."

"Staying? Staying for what? For how long?"

"For as long as it takes."

"As long as what takes? Honey, you'll never have a normal life as long as you stay there."

"What's normal?"

"Ah, now you're trying to trap me. I know your tricks. You want me to say restaurants and concerts and bookstores, but I won't."

"They don't have those things here."

"*I didn't say it!*" She waited. "I worry about you, living on that dirt road. Earning such a lousy salary. Don't think I don't admire your wonderful idealism. Everyone in the family admires your wonderful idealism, Saul, you know that. But it's like you've fallen into a cave."

"Now that could be true."

"So move out."

"I'm starting to like it."

"What's to like? Dirt? Fields? Sheep?"

"They don't have sheep here. No, I'll tell you what there is to like about it, which you would discover if you ever came to visit."

"What?"

"The indifference. Ma, I never lived with indifference before."

"*Indifference?* It's a terrible thing, kiddo."

"How would you know? You've never lived with it. Imagine people not caring that much what you do. Imagine people leaving you alone."

"A nightmare."

"You're guessing. When did people ever leave you alone? When did they ever leave *me* alone?"

"Saulie, let's not fight." She sighed dramatically. "If only you were in Detroit. You have relatives in Detroit."

"Exactly what my barber says. You been talking to him?"

"What? Your barber? What's his name?"

"Never mind. Listen, Ma, we're okay."

"Last time I talked to Patsy a couple of weeks back, she said you'd joined a bowling league." Delia waited. "You, bowling? Jews don't bowl."

"Another eleventh commandment!" Saul protested. "Rabbi Sussman used to bowl."

"He was crazy. Look what happened to him."

"Ma, you're giving me asthma. Let's not discuss this."

"Have you been to a doctor?" He replied with silence. "Honey," she said, "what am I going to say to my friends about you?"

"You can say, Saul and Patsy are getting comfortable in Michigan."

"All right, Saul. I give up. You want me to say that, that's what I'll say. Pour your life down the drain, if that's your ambition. I accept it. But let me tell you something, my friend. It's not a normal life you're leading out there."

"Okay, Ma. I'll bite, what is it?"

"It's nothing, and that's my last word on the subject. You're living in nothingness. It'll eat you up. As anyone with a brain in his head can see. But I won't interfere. Maybe nothingness suits you."

"Maybe it does."

"I can tell we aren't making progress. Goodbye, honey. I'll call again in two weeks." She made kissing noises on the mouthpiece.

"'Bye, Ma." Saul hung up the telephone in the kitchen and walked into the living room, where Patsy was watching the Sunday-afternoon movie, *From Here to Eternity*. "Take off your clothes," he said. "We're going to mess around."

She kept her eyes on the screen. "Not now. Not until this scene is over." She glanced up at him. "You must've just talked to your mother."

In the April tournament held in the Aqua Bowl, Saul scored 201, 194, and 221, and at the party afterward at Mad Dog Bettermine's summer house on the Tittebawasee River, he was exultant. Everyone had been told to bring a favorite record to the party, and Saul in an ironic mood had brought Billie Holiday's *God Bless the Child*.

Mad Dog taught shop class and coached the wrestling team; no one had ever seen him button a collar around his own neck. For the party, his statuesque girlfriend Karla had prepared two huge casseroles, one with tuna and the other with chicken, and in the back room Mad Dog was busy rolling joints packed with a powerful Colombian grown in the wet upper altitudes. All around the room on bookshelves were Mad Dog's Lionel trains, including a complete model of the Twentieth-Century Limited, with baggage car, lounge, Pullman sleepers, diner, coaches, and engine. The track had been set on top of a little red carpet. Sitting on a blue beanbag chair, Saul asked, his voice thickening with marijuana, why Mad Dog didn't run his trains on a layout but had set them up on display instead.

"These trains," Mad Dog announced, "are too *good* to run." He inhaled and inhaled and inhaled. "They're classics," he gasped. He slipped his fingers inside his shirt and started to scratch.

Saul nodded. He was wearing his bowling shirt with his name patch sewed on in front. In the next room, also thick with smoke, Patsy was dancing with Toby Finch, a fat man, as his name suggested, who taught social studies. On the other side of the room various people were tossing money on the floor as an incentive to someone to run down to the Tittebawasee River and jump into it; the money would be collected whether the daredevil wore clothes or not.

An hour later Saul's Billie Holiday record was on the turntable, and Saul himself was standing upright in the middle of the living room, a bottle of chablis in one hand, a cigarette in the other. He was singing loudly, an unpracticed baritone. "Mama may have," Saul roared, "Papa may have, but God bless the child who has his own." There was some muted applause and encouragement as Mad Dog appeared at one side of the room with another joint, and Toby appeared at the other, his clothes soaking wet, demanding cash.

"You needed a witness!" Mad Dog said. "For all we know, you went out there and wet yourself down with a garden hose."

"It's not connected," Toby said. "I tried it."

"Well, you got wet once," Saul said. "Get wet again. What's the difference? We'll watch you this time."

"Yeah," Mad Dog said. "That's right. We'll watch you jump in."

The entire party left the house and stumbled down the hillside steps, Mad Dog shushing them, until they reached the river. Half of them stood in a clump on Mad Dog's dock, while the rest gathered in the weeds and high grass just behind a small patch of sand. Toby was standing at the end of the dock, complaining of friends who doubted one's word, friends who had not taken his measure as a man and as vice-president of the Five Oaks teachers' union.

As he talked, Patsy nudged Saul in the ribs. "What about the current?" she whispered. "What about the current in the goddamn river?"

Saul offered the bottle of chablis to Patsy; she shook her head. "I asked you about the current."

Just as Toby jumped in, Saul said, "If he can survive the cold, he can survive the current." Upon hitting the water, Toby's bulk threw up a splash in all directions, wetting down those spectators on the dock. Patsy received several drops of water in her eyes, and as she wiped them away she said, "Where is he? Where's Toby?"

"He's there." Saul pointed. "Look."

Toby stood waist-deep in the Tittebawasee River, bowing to a broken round of applause. The lower buttons of his shirt had loosened, and the rolls of fat around his midsection glowed porcelain-white in the darkness. Someone threw him a dollar bill, which floated in front of him and then began drifting downstream.

"I was worried," Patsy said, turning back toward the hillside. "I thought he might drown or something."

Back in the house, someone had put on the Eagles, and then someone played the Supremes. Toby was stuffing his soaked trousers with dollar bills scattered on the floor near the kitchen, and then Saul was demonstrating how to do the tango with Patsy, and as they time-stepped across the living room, they knocked over an ashtray, and Patsy discovered she was barefoot. She couldn't remember taking her shoes off. People were applauding and laughing; someone—Mad Dog said it was Karla—was throwing up in the bathroom, and then the phonograph was playing a Vic Damone record.

Then it was three o'clock, and Saul and Patsy were at the door, Patsy's hand on Mad Dog's shoulder.

"Mad Dog," Patsy said, "you are one hundred and seventy pounds of brain death."

Mad Dog held up his index finger. "One hundred seventy-five pounds." He laughed. "Don't knock it till you've tried it."

"I've tried it," Saul said, searching the darkness for their car. "And I *love* it. Thanks, buddy. Tell Karla thanks. Great hot dish. Great party. See you Monday."

"See you," Mad Dog said. "Drive carefully."

The two of them staggered off toward the enveloping dark. Mud stuck to the soles of their shoes. At the car, Saul fiddled with his keys, trying to get at least one of them into the doorlock. "You know, pal," he said, "I love this place sometimes. I love these people."

"I know," Patsy said, leaning against the car, waiting for him, her eyes already closed. "I know."

And then they were in the car, and the car was heading south on State Highway 14, and Patsy was asleep beside Saul. Saul leaned back and pressed the CruiseControl button. He did not even realize he was shutting his eyes. He was dreaming of Patsy, sleeping within arm's reach. Patsy, whom he loved all the way down to the root. Then he was dreaming of Mrs. O'Neill, carrying a gigantic plate of chocolate chip cookies. And Bart Connell and the barber, asleep on their feet. The two red taillights of the car went around a corner that wasn't there; then one of them moved up directly above the other. Then it came down again hard, on the wrong side, and began blinking.

Media Event

✦✦

T his is his story. At the moment, he is writing it himself. He knows better than to let anyone else do it. There would be subtle gaps and distortions sewn carelessly into the fabric. He is using the third person *for greater accuracy and objectivity*. He is as objective as a cat watching a slightly damaged sparrow. Please notice: he will never make the mistake of saying "I." Right now the "I" is being doused with high-octane gasoline and set on fire, right here, where everyone can see it. "I" has been burned out. Please do not call him "I." And don't say "you," either. When you speak of him, always refer to him as "he." Or you can call him by his full name: George Eliot Christianson, Jr.

There is only one story in America, and that is the story of how to become famous. This is that story right now. Right now is 9:58 in the morning on May 20. At this moment on Channel Seven *Kelly and Company*, with its guest Danielle Gagnan Torrez, former baseball wife, is coming to an end. Thanks to this program, she is famous in southeast Michigan and will remain famous for about five hours, until dinnertime. Researcher William Wright has finished talking to John Kelly about one of the most bizarre murder cases of all time, the Claus von Bülow case. He is famous, and so is Claus von Bülow. Paul Wren, the world's strongest man (is he? Who can be sure?) lifted the show's host, John Kelly, into the air. Beauty expert Gloria Heide showed the ladies in the audience how to highlight the eyes. All these guests were on stage, exposed to public view. They sat in front of those television cameras and they appeared on his Philco set and he watched them. Over the speaker of the set came the sound of whistling and clapping of the studio audience. Now on the Donahue show George Burns is appearing. He has written an exercise book for senior citizens. He may dance and sing while holding a cigar. George Burns has been famous for a long time. He has been God and Gracie Allen's husband. *He does not need to be on television again.* He is that rare thing, a permanently famous person. He is taking up valuable air time. Someone else could be getting famous right now, instead of George Burns, on the Donahue show.

If you are not famous in America, you are considered a mistake. They suspend you in negative air and give you bad jobs working in basements pushing mops from eight at night until four in the morning. No one famous ever punches a time clock or buys no-brand niblets canned corn. If you are famous, they know how to make your face shine under the spotlights. But if you are not famous, then you are not interesting in America, and they put you in a brown uniform and you mop the Mt. Hope Hospital corridors, which is his, George Eliot Christianson, Jr.'s, job. They don't care that he wants to be somebody. Ambitions can go to Pasadena, for all the good they do. Ambitions alone are not (and will not ever be) fame.

Education means reading the books and comprehending their subtle intentions. But that doesn't make you somebody. Of course not. If it were that easy, educated people might be happy. No, you have to *write* the books and then you have to get on television. If you don't get on television you might as well eat the book page by page on a street corner. Nobody who works at the hospital with him is famous or likely to become so. If they were special, *special in any way at all*, it would be known. They would be on television, or at least on radio. It's a simple fact. Everyone knows it.

———

Contempt is visited upon the anonymous, here in our country, this America. At the department-store cashier's window they would not cash his check because he does not have a charge account with them. Without credit cards, which in the American Express commercial make you into a celebrity, he cannot rent a car. *He cannot get anyone to pay any attention to him. He is irrelevant to the world.* The world wants to erase him, inch by inch, to make room for someone who will be somebody.

There's no reason to be stupid or obscure, and there's no special reason to die like a dog in the shadows. Everyone knows it's better to shoot someone and get your name in the newspapers than to sit at home in front of the television watching other people shoot someone. The first great philosopher who suggested murder as a steppingstone to fame was Friedrich Wilhelm Nietzsche. He has read Nietzsche's philosophy and he advises his readers to do likewise. He advises reading *Menschliches, Allzumenschliches.* My God, how it re-evaluates those values. If he were alive today, Nietzsche would be a publicity agent. Or he'd be a megastar. *If Nietzsche were alive today he would not be mad.* Everyone agrees with Nietzsche now. They would have a cure for his headaches and catarrh. He'd have so many friends, he'd be a wise guy, a sage. No sweat. Who is there who hasn't at least tried to be a superman, a would-be *Übermensch?* Nietzsche invented self-promotion for our time. Behold the man.

He, George Eliot Christianson, Jr., is not going to shoot anybody. He is not a violent person, except spiritually. For him, violence is no fun. Never has been. A violent person would not work on the housekeeping staff in a hospital. He doesn't like guns or hurting other people. But he is going to be famous. One way or another.

———

Ever wonder what those girls on television get paid? The ones who appear in the toothpaste and life-insurance commercials? The ones with nothing wrong with them? They sit on a park bench and men tip their hats to them. Sorry, folks, sorry to disappoint you. As it turns out, they don't have to be paid. They're angels.

His parents were readers. They read novels in the evening after supper. In some cases, beer, tea, or coffee was served along with the novel. This bookish mode of leisure-time activity has, now, a slightly antique quality, the genteel smell of leather bindings and glue. They liked fat novels. Novels like *Middlemarch*. Like *Adam Bede*. His father worked in a sky-scraped office and his mother sometimes worked in an office and when they came home they read books to relax. They cooked gourmet dinners and then read more books, such as *Felix Holt the Radical* and *Daniel Deronda*. They named their one-and-only son after a woman, the author of those books. But they also named him after his father, who himself was named for that same woman. He was named for a woman and named for a man. It was a mad idea. *He has no name of his own.* George Eliot Christianson, Jr., is a name that has always mixed him up. Except for that "Jr." He is certain about that. It sucks, for sure.

When they moved out to the suburbs, his parents built themselves a swimming pool. What they liked best was to have the underwater lights turned on while they ate cold shrimp salad on the adjacent deck, and drank white wine, and discussed their investments. From the pool came the turquoise glow of the painted water waved by the evening wind, and George Sr. would look at it and say, "Somehow it reminds me of a Japanese painting."

"It reminds *me*," his wife would say, "of water in the Caribbean."

George Eliot Christianson, Jr., home for the evening, sitting with them, eating his scanty dinner, keeps a respectful distance, a proud silence during this monstrous colloquy.

"George," George says, "do you have any plans for changing your job?" His father looks at him with that look.

"No," George says.

"Well," George says, "maybe it's time to *start* thinking about it. Maybe it's time to start making something of yourself."

"Yes." The theme is the pool; he is the subject.

"We—your mother and I—are often asked what our son is doing and we have to tell them that he's a janitor in a hospital. I know your mother sometimes just doesn't tell them at all."

"I'm on the housekeeping staff," George says. "I'm not a janitor. There's a difference. They fix it. We keep it clean."

"Oh, George," his mother says, turning to him, "let's not talk about this tonight. Let's have a nice dinner." Her face is lit by the rippling and flickering blue waves in the pool.

"I must say," George says, "I am sometimes annoyed by your obstinance. I know your sisters are puzzled, as I am. Here you are, a young man with all the advantages: intelligence, and a good education. *You had no defects.* And yet, look. What happened to you? You will not play the game. You *insist* on ruining your prospects. I remember the hippies, and perhaps it is the fashion again to spite us and all that we stand for. I cannot believe that a young man with a college degree would *want* to work in a hospital, however. Is a secure life with a solid income so shameful a thing? Why don't you wish to make something of yourself?"

"Hmmmm," George says.

"I hate to think that you'll never find your peg, your niche. I hate to think that you'll spend your life being strange."

And then he, George Eliot Christianson, Jr., awakens, and looks toward his father, and says, "I am *not* strange. I am a product of this society, just as you are. I just don't have your idea of swimming pools as wondrous objects of beauty." And he stands up, and takes his plate of shrimp salad, and his wineglass, and drops them into the water of the swimming pool.

For the first time in the evening his mother screams.

Now he is back in his apartment sitting on the bed. He has driven home in his unsafe-at-any-speed Pontiac Astre. He is staring out his sooty apartment window at the King Koil factory, which is almost in his backyard. Here is what he sees: brownish brick, interrupted every seven feet by high windows with translucent glass, open, and bare light bulbs visible inside. Here is what he hears: incessant rhythmic clatter. Here is what he smells: the odor of hot metals, and grease, and metallic dust, and paint. Black smoke emerges from the chimney, environmentally protected smoke, rubs its muzzle on the windowpanes, and slips inside his room, where it burns his throat with the soulful righteous waste of manufactured bedsprings.

He'll draw you a picture, a vacation from sitting on the bed and looking out the window at the bedspring factory. Here's the picture. Waterskiing! People in swimsuits. It's a lake, let's say in Wisconsin, where the water has temporarily escaped acid rain and where the houses on shore have been designed so that you can't see them from the water. They blend in. That cosmetic feature costs extra in exterior natural wood paneling, but it's worth it. In this picture three people are happy. There's this man, Freddy Emerson. There's his girlfriend, Tracy Edwards, whom everyone calls Trace. And there's George Eliot Christianson, Jr., whom everyone calls George. Freddy and Trace are substantially beautiful in the midsummer sun. They both have the copyrighted suntans of the youthful leisure class. Freddy is behind the wheel of the powerful outboard and Trace is sitting in the backseat, watching. Who's going to be up on skis? George is, that's who. He's up now, the future disappointment to the serious world, skimming over the lake. *He is on one ski!* And, like Freddy and Trace, he is physically picturesque. All three of these people are eighteen years old. Two of them admire George as he slashes back and forth across a slalom course of blue anchored plastic bottles. The future hospital housekeeper is very very impressive, a golden Aztec sungod. The sun has baked his hair so that it's quite blond. Looking down into the water, he can see fish, several feet below the surface, swimming in a neutral manner. But really he is being pulled too fast to see much of the fish or even the sun as it is reflected on the water. He's much too happy to notice things. He's a decisive water-skier. If it were his own boat he'd be even better, but it's Freddy Emerson's father's Alumacraft, his father's Evinrude outboard, and Trace is Freddy Emerson's girl. She is privately held.

Well. Imagine yourself up on that one slalom ski, in that lake in Wisconsin. Then say to yourself: if that was ten, or even fifteen years ago, what visions of sunlight have been his share since that time? What happens to sunlight in the complicated culture of postcapitalist America? What has happened since they snuffed the summer sun and Trace took off her swimsuit and put on her power clothes for her job in the office on the ninth floor where she draws down $47K per year? What has happened to George and his happiness? Stay tuned. How does a man keep on falling through the water until he becomes one of the fish?

"Oh dear." You look up. "Another story about a maladjusted person. Another flake. Another weirdo. What a shame."

Dear reader, George Eliot Christianson, Jr., is an extremely relevant person. He stands up for the stupid and crazy. He is a spokesperson for those sucked out of comfort into odd rented rooms, shacks, and messy walkups. Why, *you've got one like him in your own family.* Your brother's son. Your own daughter. Your cousin, who couldn't hold a job. Your uncle, who keeps having accidents with his damaged hands and whose bills are paid by the family. Your husband, who sits at home. Your grandchild, who isn't turning out right. Your own blood, your genes, your genetic pool. Your wife, your mother. You.

Don't you goddamn dare pretend he's so strange.

How *did* George Eliot Christianson, Jr., who earned a B.A. *magna cum laude* from a fine college in Massachusetts and whose habitual prose style was not unremarkable and whose prospects were, as they say, bright, how did this promising young man from the deep midwest, this little lamb without a spot, how did he manage so forcefully to crash the car of his career into a solid void? No, it's a dull question and he won't answer. Look around: astonishing quantities of also-rans in all walks of life, God's plenty of failure. No scarcity. Do you think it's unusual that a man of astrostellar potential should be pushing a mop down a hospital corridor? Half the underclass in this country could competently staff the Sorbonne. Here's what happened: George Eliot Christianson, Jr., took a slight psychic tumble. He fell into a bit of depression about himself and his ultimate human prospects here in this, our, America. He got depressed, and so did the economy. It's a free country if you have a million dollars, but if you don't and you're a little discouraged about things, you take what they give you. At Mt. Hope they were passing out mops. He took one.

The woman is sitting on the edge of his mattress. She is naked and she is smoking a Camel Lite and complaining about the view. "George," she says, flicking out her hair with her other hand, "I don't mind that you have paper window shades. And I don't mind that they're ripped." She exhales some smoke and scratches her instep. "But what I *do* mind is the noise of the factory and what I mind even more is that when we do it in this room you do it in time with the noise of those stamping machines. Boom. Boom. Boom. Boom. Boom." She transfers the cigarette to the other hand and lowers her long painted fingernails to his chest. "You're kind of sweet, sometimes, but when we go at it in this room I feel like I'm mating with an android." She reaches down for an empty Coke bottle and flicks the ash from the cigarette into it. "Oh," she says. "One other thing. I wish you'd buy some furniture. *One* chair won't make you part of the bourgeoisie. Even revolutionaries eat their meals at tables." She drops the cigarette into the Coke bottle, and it makes a hollow hiss.

The sum and substance of being on the housekeeping staff in a modern hospital is what now follows. Being new (1976), the hospital is dressed and decorated in tranquilized earth tones of copper, brown, speckled rust, and tan: the reassuring and antiprimary end of the spectrum. He himself dresses each night in a locker room where he puts on his antiprimary uniform of deepest darkest institutional brown. He has his own special housekeeping cart, labeled C-7. At one end of his cart is the bucket filled with Huntington Hi-Tor Germicidal Detergent, and, of course, the water. The bucket also contains a wringer for draining one's mop, which bucket is bolted to the aforementioned end of the cart. His job is regularly to mop the basement and ground-floor hallways and once a week to wax them with Huntington's Hospital-Industrial Floor Wax and to use the General Electric buffer on those floors, not once but twice, according to housekeeping regulations. But he is not finished describing cart C-7 and its contents. He must clean the bathrooms. Bathrooms constitute a special problem. They must be mopped, of course, and the red liquid soap—Huntington Germa-Medica "R"—must be poured into the hand-soap dispensers. If these dispensers are clogged, the men from maintenance must declog them. He must wash and rinse the sinks and toilets and spray the mirrors and walls with Compass Germicide and Deodorant, in its red-and-white can, another little passenger on his cart. Gum underneath the sink? It must be removed, *and he must do it,* with his spray can of Claire chewing-gum remover with the special long-nosed nozzle. When he cleans out the gift shop he must vacuum the brown polyester carpet using the Hoover purchased from Ask Tidy Tom Services, Inc. Certain porcelain surfaces must be scrubbed with one's cleaning rag and Liquid Por-San. When no one is looking, he does something he is not authorized to do: he dusts the faces of the clocks set into the walls at fifty-foot intervals. You always know what time it is in a hospital. He must pick up all refuse and put it in his clear polyvinyl-chloride bag, which will eventually be noosed with ribbon wire and transported to the dumpster on the north side of the building. During coffee break he steps outside and with his co-workers Jim Ripley and Joanne Ash he sucks into his lungs several hits of the potentest Colombian that a laborer's wages can search out and score. Then he blithely reenters the building, where, because it is modern, the hallways meet at acute or obtuse angles. Only on the surgical floor can lines be found that meet at 90 degrees. At four o'clock in the morning he has done one man's penance and passed through another working night and he is ready to punch out. All night he has held in his nostrils the smell of soap and sickness, and that smell is now nesting under his fingernails. He knows by heart the odor of the ailing disfigured physical body. It is that smell that enters his dreams, not the recessed lighting or the enclosed garden courtyards or the nurses' stations. He goes home and in his bed where Sandra-the-cigarette-smoker also sometimes sleeps he dreams of acres and acres of rotting orchards where the fruit smells of disease and soap.

Sometimes he feels the wind blowing inside his fingers. Yes, *inside.*

——

We know about Oswald and Ray, but who remembers Sara Jane Moore, or Squeaky Fromme, who had nothing against Gerald Ford, or Mark David Chapman, who had nothing against John Lennon, or John Hinckley, Jr., who had nothing against Ronald Reagan? They weren't just typographical errors. *They weren't exceptions.* They found guns and went looking for someone famous to shoot. Oh. He almost forgot. Arthur Bremer. And his line as he pulled the trigger: "A penny for your thoughts."

Any man who has imagination must resist servitude; he must learn how to turn himself into a terrible risk.

We all agree that everybody wants to be somebody. We all agree that that is where the pressure is applied here in America and where they turn up the spiritual thermostat. The problem with fame is that the means to achieve it cross into insanity and criminality. If they lock you up, your fame is useless, for the most part.

Who really wants to be in *The Guinness Book of World Records*? Is that a sensible way to achieve selfhood? Who really wants to go bowling for two days without stopping until the fingertips are bleeding and the knuckles are so swollen that they've become useless? Who wants to do this just to get into *The Guinness Book*? Who wants to sit on a ledge for eight days or eat twenty cherry pies in a row or fall two thousand feet from a speeding orthogyro just to get into that book? No, *The Guinness Book* is a record of failed acts of the imagination, notable only for their duration.

What about interrupting Vladimir Horowitz? Suppose Vladimir Horowitz is performing Beethoven's Fourth Piano Concerto with Zubin Mehta and the New York Philharmonic. He is performing in his usual style. The auditorium is oozing with rapture at his "magnetism" and "dynamic power." Beethoven is forgotten. What is exciting is Horowitz. It's time to put a stop to this travesty of musicianship. Who does it? You do. You stand up and you cry, "Stop this grandstand meddling with the classics!" You might even go up to the stage and forcibly remove Horowitz. Result? You will be famous, the first man to have stopped Horowitz in that gentleman's long career of murdering the classics. Some will admire you. Much good their admiration will do you, in your cell. This cell will be padded, because you will be crazy without appeal, because in this society the very definition of sanity is *completely* associated with staying hushed at symphony concerts, especially those at which Vladimir Horowitz deigns to appear. Just *try* to find a psychiatrist who doesn't love Vladimir Horowitz. "I may not like you," the psychiatrist who is examining you with his tweezers says, "but I *love* Vladimir Horowitz."

Two weeks ago he was bicycling to work. He had to stop at an intersection for a red light. He looked around, gazing at the urban intersected world. An apartment building. Second floor, corner window. A man in an undershirt, his back to the street, sitting next to a highchair. He was spooning cereal into the baby's mouth. His wife across the table was watching. A picture of calm, of peacefulness. George Eliot Christianson, Jr., sitting on his bicycle, felt the two hands of implacable fate gathering around his heart, and as those two hands squeezed he looked down into the gutter and saw an ant carrying a piece of cracker. You can look all you want. But if you're being erased, it'll make you feel like a man in a maelstrom.

What will lead him out of the maelstrom and the hospital where he works as a mere housekeeper into the limelight, where everyone is a star, and therefore happy? He knows what will capture the imagination of the public. He will no longer tease you with his project. Here is what he is going to do. He is going to walk through plate glass.

———

He remembers his boyhood dog, Sonny, and some good dinners. He remembers good sex. Well, fine. These memories—he too drank Kool-Aid, he too went to the beach—do not minimize the turned-up tension of his anonymity. Take him outside. Show him the sun. Explain the name of that tree. Praise the grass. Then praise the sky and note for the one millionth time in your life that it's blue. Will such praise cure his spiritual ache? Has such praise ever worked with your weird uncle, or your daughter who turned out bad, or your brother the unemployed beer drinker? Ever sermonize to them about the sun? They don't even look at you, do they?

He stands at the window, then walks to the kitchen. He takes down a glass and fills it with water. He drinks the water, then sits down on a pillow in the living room. He checks the view. He scratches his left shoulder. He stands up. He touches the wall. He walks into the bedroom, then back out of it. He sees through the window a time-and-temperature clock in the distance. 2:57. Blink. 61°. He thinks of the other insomniacs and those possessed by intolerable longings, and he thinks of them all, wandering from room to room, a little army writing the natural history of the waking night.

Of course Sandra-the-cigarette-smoker thinks the typewriter project is a joke. He must be writing this up to improve his typing skills for a possible clerical job. Well: there he is, sitting (in a chair, Sandra, *in a chair!*) at this very desk day after day, she believes, to while away the working-class leisure hours. She thinks that if she were to put her long arms around his neck and insert her tongue in his ear and so on and so on, he'd be okay. The desk is cluttered with pencils, coffee cups, and a dictionary of synonyms to fulfill a hobby, she thinks. *No one walks through plate glass.* Come on, give her a break. Not her guy George. Through plate glass? And ruin his face? And cut himself? Where's the logic?

Plate glass.

Well, it's obvious. It keeps you out and them in, pretends it's not a wall, *can* be broken by human force, lets you see what you want but keeps you from having it, *is* the stoned face of every television set in the land, and is made of sand and built with fire and lets us look but not touch.

What goes on behind plate glass?

In their own rooms, soft with plush decorations, live the lucky ones, with souls. They sleep at night. Daytimes, they walk on sidewalks headed for some destination. Their children laugh musically. Ha ha ha. Their landscapes are shockingly green. The seasons arrive on time and leaves follow blossoms and are themselves followed faithfully by fruit. Their airwaves shake to the sound of arguing birds, and there, there in the distance, is an incognito mountain. Green meadows, anonymous slopes. Here are baskets of bread and cheese. Drink and eat.

Well, okay, it's true that that mountain may be a little sentimental, but it's not a golden mountain, it's not imaginary, he's seen the pictures, his parents have been there, and so have his friends, and they brought back presents, bottles of white wine.

Sometimes he thinks he is making a terrible mistake. He looks over what he has written so far and thinks: oh, this can't be right, this is awful. They'll look at him and say, the man didn't know what he was doing. A self-intoxicant. A media hound.

The doubts don't go away. Why isn't Sandra's body enough?

And he steps forward. His Adidas tennis shoes give him considerable momentum. His forehead touches the glass first, then his left shoulder. A moment of resistance. Then. Then a crack, a crackling, a spider web of splitting sections. And the sun splits, and then it's raining knives and daggers and icicles.

And he stands in this rain, a brief summer shower of glass. He keeps his eyes closed as he begins to bleed, and he's happy.

Q: Which plate glass?

A: The front window of the First Manufacturers Trust.

Q: Is it thick?

A: Quite thick. But it can be walked through.

Q: How do you know?

A: He knows because someone once walked through it by accident, so they put a green painted line on it so no one would walk through it again.

Q: What injuries will you sustain?

A: That is a big question mark. It depends on the speed and the angle of entry. There are likely to be severe lacerations on the forehead and arms and probably·on the shoulders, which will be the first actually to emerge on the other side of the glass.

Q: What if the glass cannot be broken?

A: That is unimaginable.

Q: Why the Manufacturers Trust?

A: It's a bank. His puny checking account is there. Banks represent for him and for most people the seat of plate-glass power. People *want* to break through, into, banks. Happiness is held secret in their huge vaults.

Q: Does anyone know you will be doing it?

A: He has called Channel Two, Channel Four, and Channel Seven and told them to have their news crews out in front of the bank at two-thirty p.m. He has mailed three different *but highly articulate* rationales, over which he has spent uncounted hours, to the stations. Once in the hospital, he will set up interviews like this one and begin writing.

Q: Which hospital?

A: Mt. Hope. They know him there.

Q: You *do* expect injuries?

A: Everything has its price. There'll be some loss of blood. Not to worry.

Q: What will you write?

A: The plate-glass statement. The last word on the subject.

Q: Do you regard yourself as a victim, a loser?

A: I regard myself as a hero, a winner.

Q: What will your friends, parents, associates think?

A: They have not been informed. They will understand, in time.

In a few hours, he will be famous. At least you have to admit that he's thought this through; you have to say, "He *has* his reasons." Many others might do the same, given the right circumstances. If everyone has the right to be famous for fifteen minutes, you have to admit that *now is the time*. He speaks for many. This is an army. Their numbers are growing. They are churning their way into the public eye, by God. Sometimes they are violent. But *no one is going to be hurt here*, except for him, a bit. But he'll come out flying. It's a small price to pay for a picnic on a mountain, for a real name in this unreal world.

Go ahead. Wish him luck. Be polite.

Surprised by Joy

1

Because their psychiatrist had recommended it, they both began to keep journals. Jeremy's was Woolworth-stationery drab, and Harriet's was sea-blue with the words "A Blank Book" printed in gold script in the upper right-hand corner. Thinking that pleasant images would relieve the tone of what was to follow, she sketched a wren in flight, a Victorian lamp-post, and an ash tree on the first page. Then she changed her mind and blacked the drawings out. There weren't any drawings in the book Jeremy used. His writing was tiny and defiant. His first sentence, which was undated, read: "Benson told us it would help if we wrote down our thoughts, but I don't have any thoughts, and besides, the fact is that I don't feel like writing a goddamn thing." That was the end of the first entry.

One night Jeremy came home and found all the silverware—knives, forks, spoons, gravy bowls, and ladles—lined up according to type on the living-room carpet in front of the hide-a-bed sofa. Harriet said she wanted to do an inventory, to make sure the place settings were all present and accounted for. She threatened to count all the dishes, and all the books. A week later when he arrived home she was standing on her head with her legs crossed and her knees positioned against the wall. He put down his briefcase, hung up his coat, and sat in his chair. "So," he said. "What's this?"

"An article I read says it helps." Upside down, she attempted a smile.

"Standing on your head."

"Yeah. Think about it: the brain under stress needs more blood, the cerebral cortex especially. The article says that when you stand up you feel an instant of physical exhilaration." She closed her eyes. "The plumber came out this morning. The faucet's fixed."

"Physical exhilaration." He turned away from her to stare out at the street, where two children were roaring by on their Big Wheels.

"They say you'll feel better."

"Right. What article did you say this was?" He didn't wait for her to answer. "It sounds like *Parade* magazine. How much did the plumber charge? God, I could use a drink. I have the most amazing willpower." He glanced at her. "Did you cry a lot today?"

"No. Not much. Not like last week. I even did two full baskets of laundry. After lunch, when the plumber was gone, that was hard. For about ten minutes I couldn't help it and locked myself in the bathroom and then I wrote in the journal. Gretchen called and invited me into her weaving class. Do you think I should? It seems so dull and womanish. How was your day?" She tumbled backward, stood up, and looked at him with an unsteady, experimental smile.

"Do you feel exhilarated?" She shrugged. He said, "I feel the usual. Carrying around the black box." He rose, went to the kitchen for a beer, and clomped down the stairs to the basement, where he played his clarinet while watching television with the sound off. His music consisted of absentminded riffs in eerie unrelated keys.

They had brought their child home to a plain three-bedroom brick bungalow of the type referred to as a "starter house" for young married couples. Its distinguishing characteristics were those left by the previous owners. Jeremy and Harriet had never had time to redecorate it; as a result, their bedroom was covered with flocked jungle-orange wallpaper, the paint in Harriet's sewing room was oyster-gray, and the child's room had been painted blue, with two planets and four constellations mapped out on the ceiling with phosphorus dots and circles. At the time, their child was too little to notice such things: she gurgled at the trees outside and at the birds that sang in the shrubbery below her windowsill.

This child, Ellen, had been born after many difficulties. Harriet had had a series of ovarian cysts. She ovulated irregularly and only when provoked by certain powerful hormonal medications that left her so forgetful that she had to draw up hourly schedules for the day's tasks. She had the scars to prove that surgical procedures had been used to remove her enlarged ovaries piece by piece. The baby had been in a troublesome position, and Harriet had endured sixteen hours of labor, during which time she thrashed and groaned. Jeremy watched her lying in the hospital gown, his hands pressed against her lower back, while her breathing grew louder, hoarse and rhythmical. Their Lamaze lessons proved to be useless. The lights glared overhead in the prep room and could not be dimmed. In its labors her body heaved as if her reproductive system were choking in its efforts to expel the child. Her obstetrician was out of town on vacation in Puerto Vallarta, so the delivery was finally performed by a resident, a young woman who had a short hairdo and whose purple fingernail polish was visible through her surgical gloves.

The oyster-gray paint and the phosphorus planets in the house suited Ellen, who, when she was old enough to toddle, would point at the stars on the ceiling and wave at them. At this time she could not pronounce her own name and referred to herself as "Ebbo" or, mysteriously, as "Purl." On a spring morning she climbed from the crib onto the windowsill in pursuit of a chickadee singing outside. Cheered by the sun, Harriet had left the window open to let the breeze in. Ellen pushed herself past the sill and managed to tumble out, breaking the screen. She landed on a soft newly tilled flower bed next to a bush. When Harriet found her, she was tugging at flower shoots and looking pleased with herself. She said, "Purl drop." She shrugged her right shoulder and smiled.

They latched the screen onto a stronger frame and rushed around the house looking for hazards. They installed a lock on the basement door so she wouldn't tumble downstairs, and fastened shut the kitchen sink's lower cabinet so she wouldn't eat the ElectraSol. She lived one day past her third Christmas, when for the first time she knew what a Christmas tree was and could look forward to it with dazed anticipation. On Christmas Day she was buried up to her waist in presents: a knee-high table complete with cups and saucers, Bert and Ernie finger dolls, a plastic Fisher-Price phonograph, a stuffed brown bear that made wheezing sounds, a Swiss music box, a windup train that went around in a small circle, a yellow toy police car with a lady cop inside, and, in her stocking, pieces of candy, gum, a comb, and a red rubber ball her mother had bought at Kiddie Land for twenty-five cents.

On December 26, Jeremy and Harriet were slumped in the basement, watching Edmund Gwenn in *Miracle on 34th Street* for the eighth or ninth time, while Ellen played upstairs in her room. They went through three commercial breaks before Harriet decided to check on her. She hadn't been worried because she could hear the Fisher-Price phonograph playing a Sesame Street record. Harriet went down the hallway and turned the corner into Ellen's room. Her daughter was lying on the floor, on her side, her skin blue. She wasn't breathing. On her forehead was blood next to a bright cut. Harriet's first thought was that Ellen had somehow been knocked unconscious by an intruder. Then she was shouting for Jeremy, and crying, and touching Ellen's face with her fingers. She picked her up, pounded her back, and then felt the lump of the red rubber ball that Ellen had put in her mouth and that had lodged in her throat. She squeezed her chest and the ball came up into the child's mouth.

Jeremy rushed in behind her. He took Ellen away from Harriet and carried her into the living room, her arms hanging down, swinging. He shouted instructions at Harriet. Some made sense; others didn't. He gave Ellen mouth-to-mouth resuscitation and kept putting his hand against her heart, waiting for a pulse.

Later they understood that Ellen had panicked and had run into the edge of the open closet door. What with the movie and the new phonograph, they hadn't heard her. The edge of the door wasn't sharp, but she had run into it so blindly that the collision had dazed her. She had fallen and reached up to her forehead: a small amount of blood had dried on her hands. She had then reached for her stuffed raccoon; her left hand was gripping its leg. She was wearing, for all time, her yellow Dr. Denton pajamas. In the living room, waiting for the ambulance, Harriet clutched her own hands. Then she was drinking glass after glass of water in a white waiting room.

Their parents said, oh, they could have another, a child as beautiful as Ellen. Her doctors disagreed. Harriet's ovaries had been cut away until only a part of one of them remained. In any case, they didn't want replacements. The idea made no sense. What they thought of day and night was what had happened upstairs while they were watching television. Their imaginations put the scene on a film loop. Guiltily, they watched it until their mental screens began to wash the rest of the past away.

For the next two months they lived hour to hour. Every day became an epic of endurance, in which Harriet sat in chairs. Harriet's mother called every few days, offering excruciating maternal comfort. There were photographs, snapshots and studio portraits that neither of them could stand to remove. Nature became Harriet's enemy. She grew to hate the sun and its long lengthening arcs. When living trees broke open into pink and white blossoms in the spring, Harriet wanted to fling herself against them. She couldn't remember what it was about life that had ever interested her. The world began a vast and buzzing commentary to keep her in cramps, preoccupied with Ellen, who had now irresistibly become Purl. The grass no longer grew up from the ground but instead stood as a witless metaphor of continuing life. Dishes and silverware upset her, unaccountably. She couldn't remember who her friends were and did not recognize them in the street. Every night the sky fell conclusively.

Jeremy had his job, but every evening, after seeing about Harriet, he went straight down to the basement where the television set was. He played his clarinet, drank beer, and watched *Hogan's Heroes* and the local news until it was time for dinner. He opened the twist-top beer bottles and drank the beer mechanically, as if acting on orders. After overhearing the music he played, Harriet began to call it "jazz from Mars," and Jeremy said, yes, that was probably where it came from. He paid attention to things at work; his music could afford to be inattentive.

He came upstairs when dinner was ready. This meal consisted of whatever food Harriet could think of buying and preparing. They didn't like to go out. They often ate hot dogs and A&P potato salad, or hamburger, or pizza delivered by the Domino's man in a green Gremlin. Jeremy sometimes fell asleep at the dinner table, his head tilted back at the top of the chair, and his mouth open, sucking in breaths. Harriet would drape one of his arms around her neck and lower him to the floor, so he wouldn't fall off the chair while asleep. They had talked about getting chairs with arms to prevent accidents of this kind; they both assumed they would spend the rest of their lives falling asleep at the table after dinner.

They started seeing Benson, the therapist, because of what happened with the Jehovah's Witnesses. In mid-May, the doorbell rang just after dinner. Jeremy, who this time was still awake, rose from the table to see who it was. Outside the screen door stood a red-haired man and a small red-haired boy, eight or nine years old, dressed in nearly identical gray coats and bow ties. The father was carrying a copy of *Awake!* and *The Watchtower*. The boy held a Bible, a children's edition with a crude painting of Jesus on the cover. Leaving the screen door shut, Jeremy asked them what they wanted.

"My son would like to read to you," the man said, glancing down at the boy. "Do you have time to listen for a minute?"

Jeremy said nothing.

Taking this as a sign of agreement, the man nodded at the boy, who pushed his glasses back, opened the Bible, and said, "Psalm forty-three." He swallowed, looked up at his father, who smiled, then pulled at the red silk bookmark he had inserted at the beginning of the psalm. He cleared his throat. "Give sentence with me, O God," he read, his finger trailing horizontally along the line of type, his voice quavering, "and defend my cause against the ungodly people; O deliver me from the deceitful and wicked man." He stumbled over "deceitful." The boy paused and looked through the screen at Jeremy. Jeremy was watching the boy with the same emptied expression he used when watching television. His father touched the boy on the shoulder and told him to continue. A bird was singing nearby. Jeremy looked up. It was a cardinal on a telephone wire.

"For thou art the God of my strength," the boy read. "Why hast thou put me from thee? and why go I so heavily, while the enemy oppresseth me?"

For the first time, Jeremy said something. He said, "I don't believe it. You can't be doing this." The father and the boy, however, didn't hear him. The boy continued.

"O send out thy light and thy truth, that they may lead me, and bring me unto thy holy hill, and to thy dwelling."

Jeremy said, "Who sent you here?" The father heard what he said, but his only reaction was to squint through the screen to see Jeremy better. He gave off a smell of cheap after-shave.

"And that I may go unto the altar of God," the boy read, "even unto the God of my joy and gladness; and upon the harp will I give thanks unto thee, O God, my God."

"You're contemptible," Jeremy said, "to use children. That's a low trick."

This time both the boy and his father stared in at him. Harriet had appeared and was standing behind Jeremy, pulling at his shirt and whispering instructions to him to thank them and send them on their merry way. The father, however, recovered himself, smiled, pointed at the Bible, and then touched his son on the head, as if pressing a button.

"Why art thou so heavy, O my soul?" the boy read, stuttering slightly. "And why art thou so disquieted within me?"

"Stop it!" Jeremy shouted. "Please stop it! Stop it!" He opened the screen door and walked out to the front stoop so that he was just to the right of the father and his boy. Harriet crossed her arms but otherwise could not or did not move. Jeremy reached up and held on to the man's lapel. He didn't grab it but simply put it between his thumb and forefinger. He aimed his words directly into the center of the father's face. "Who sent you here?" he asked, his words thrown out like stones. "This was no accident. Don't tell me this was an accident, because I'd hate to think you were lying to me. Someone sent you here. Right? Who? How'd they ever think of using kids?" The bird was still singing, and when Jeremy stopped he heard it again, but hearing it only intensified his anger. "You want to sell me *The Watchtower*?" he asked, sinking toward inarticulateness. Then he recovered. "You want my money?" He let go of the man's lapel, reached into his pocket, and threw a handful of nickels and dimes to the ground. "Now go away and leave me alone."

The stranger was looking at Jeremy, and his mouth was opening. The boy was clutching his father's coat. One of the dimes was balanced on his left shoe.

"Go home," Jeremy said, "and never say another word about anything and don't ever again knock on my door." Jeremy was a lawyer. When speeches came to him, they came naturally. His face in its rage was as white as paper. He stopped, looked down, and hurriedly kissed the boy on the top of the head. As he straightened up, he said softly, "Don't mind me." Then, mobilized, Harriet rushed out onto the stoop and grabbed Jeremy's hand. She tried smiling.

"You see that my husband's upset," she said, pulling at him. "I think you should go now."

"Yes, all right," the father mumbled, blinking, taking the Bible from his son and closing it. The air thickened with the smell of his after-shave.

"We've had an accident recently," she explained. "We weren't prepared."

The man had his arm around his son's shoulders. They were starting down the walk to the driveway. "The Bible is a great comfort," the man said over his shoulder. "A help ever sure." He stopped to look back. "Trust in God," he said.

Jeremy made a roaring sound, somewhere between a shout and a bark, as Harriet hauled him back inside.

Benson's office was lodged on the twentieth floor of a steel-and-glass professional building called the Kelmer Tower. After passing through Benson's reception area, a space not much larger than a closet, the patient stepped into Benson's main office, where the sessions were actually conducted. It was decorated in therapeutic pastels, mostly off-whites and pale blues. Benson had set up bookshelves, several chairs, and a couch, and had positioned a rubber plant near the window. In front of the chairs was a coffee table on which was placed, not very originally, a small statue of a Minotaur. Benson's trimmed mustache and otherworldly air made him look like a wine steward. He had been recommended to them by their family doctor, who described Benson as a "very able man."

Harriet thought Benson was supposed to look interested; instead, he seemed bored to the point of stupefaction. He gave the appearance of thinking of something else: baseball, perhaps, or his golf game. Several times, when Jeremy was struggling to talk, Benson turned his face away and stared out the window. Harriet was afraid that he was going to start humming Irving Berlin songs. Instead, when Jeremy was finished, Benson looked at him and asked, "So. What are you going to do?"

"Do? Do about what?"

"Those feelings you've just described."

"Well, what am I supposed to do?"

"I don't think there's anything you're supposed to do. It's a choice. If you want me to recommend something, I can recommend several things, among them that you keep a journal, a sort of record. But you don't have to."

"That's good." Jeremy looked down at the floor, where the slats of sunlight through the venetian blinds made a picket fence across his feet.

"If you don't want my help," Benson said, "you don't have to have it."

"At these prices," Jeremy said, "I want something."

"Writing in a journal can help," Benson continued, "because it makes us aware of our minds in a concrete way." Harriet cringed over Benson's use of the paternal first-person plural. She looked over at Jeremy. He was gritting his teeth. His jaw muscles were visible in his cheek. "Crying helps," Benson told them, and suddenly Harriet was reminded of the last five minutes of Captain Kangaroo, the advice part. "And," Benson said slowly, "it helps to get a change of scene. Once you're ready and have the strength and resources to do it, you might try going on a trip."

"Where?" Harriet asked.

"Where?" Benson looked puzzled. "Why, anywhere. Anywhere that doesn't look like this. Try going to someplace where the scenery is different. Nassau. Florida. Colorado."

"How about the Himalayas?" Jeremy asked.

"Yes," Benson said, not bothering to act annoyed. "That would do."

They both agreed that they might be able to handle it if it weren't for the dreams. Ellen appeared in them and insisted on talking. In Jeremy's dreams, she talked about picnics and hot dogs, how she liked the catsup on the opposite side of the wiener from the mustard, and how she insisted on having someone toast the bun. The one sentence Jeremy remembered with total clarity when he woke up was: "Don't *like* soggy hot dogs." He wouldn't have remembered it if it hadn't sounded like her.

She was wearing a flannel shirt and jeans in Jeremy's dream; in Harriet's she had on a pink jumper that Harriet had bought for her second birthday. Harriet saw that she was outgrowing it. With a corkscrew feeling she saw that Ellen was wearing a small ivory cameo with her own—Harriet's—profile on it. She was also wearing a rain hat that Harriet couldn't remember from anywhere, and she was carrying a Polaroid photograph of her parents. Harriet wondered vaguely how dead children get their hands on such pictures. In this dream Harriet was standing on a street corner in a depopulated European city where the shutters were all closed tight over the windows. Near her, overhead in the intersection, the traffic light hanging from a thick cable turned from green to amber to red, red to green, green to amber to red. However, no cars charged through the intersection, and no cars were parked on the street. A rhythmic thud echoed in the streets. Leaves moldered in the gutters. Harriet knew that it was a bad city for tourists. In this place Ellen scampered toward her down the sidewalk, wearing the pink jumper and the rain hat, the photograph in her hand, the cameo pinned near her collar. She smiled. Harriet stumbled toward her, but Ellen held out her hand and said, "Can't hug." Harriet asked her about the hat, and Ellen said, "Going to rain." She looked up at the bleary sky, and, following her lead, so did Harriet. Flocks of birds flew from left to right across it in no special pattern, wing streaks of indecision. Clouds. Harriet gazed down at Ellen. "Are you okay?" Harriet asked. "Who's taking care of you?" Ellen was picking her nose. "Lots of people," she said, wiping her finger on her pant leg. "They're nice." "Are you all right?" Harriet asked again. Ellen lifted her right shoulder. "Yeah," she said. She looked up. "Miss you, Mommy," she said, and, against directions, Harriet bent down to kiss her, wanting the touch of her skin against her lips, but when she reached Ellen's face, Ellen giggled, looked around quickly as if she were being watched from behind the shuttered windows, reached both hands up to cover her mouth, and disappeared, leaving behind a faint odor of flowers.

"Such dreams are common," Benson said. "Very very common."

"Tell me something else," Harriet said.

"What do you want me to tell you?"

"Something worth all the money we're paying you."

"You sound like Jeremy. What *would* be worth all the money you're paying me?"

"I have the feeling," Harriet said, "that you're playing a very elaborate game with us. And you have more practice at it than we do."

"If it's a game," Benson said, "then I do have more practice. But if it's not a game, I don't." He waited. Harriet stared at the giant leaves of the rubber plant, standing in the early-summer light, torpid and happy. Jeremy hadn't come with her this time. The Minotaur on the coffee table looked inquisitive. "What is the dream telling you about Ellen, do you think?"

"That she's all right?"

"Yes." Benson breathed out. "And what do you have to worry about?"

"Not Ellen."

"No, not Ellen. The dream doesn't say to worry about her. So what do you have to worry about?"

"Jeremy. I don't see him. And I have to worry about getting out of that city."

"Why should you worry about Jeremy?"

"I don't know," Harriet said. "He's hiding somewhere. I want to get us both out of that city. It gives me the creeps."

"Yes. And how are you going to get out of that city?"

"Run?" Harriet looked at Benson. "Can I run out of it?"

"If you want to." Benson thought for a moment. "If you want to, you will run out of it." He smoothed his tie. "But you can't run and pull Jeremy at the same time."

After Jeremy's dream, she no longer served hot dogs for dinner. That night she was serving pork chops, and when Jeremy came in, still in his vest but with his coat over his shoulder, she was seated at the table, looking through a set of brochures she had picked up at a travel agency down the block from Benson's office. After Jeremy had showered and changed his clothes, he was about to take a six-pack out of the refrigerator when he looked over at Harriet studying a glossy photograph of tourists riding mules on Molokai. "It says here," Harriet announced, "in this brochure, that Molokai is the flattest of all the islands and the one with the most agricultural activity."

"Are you going on a quiz show? Is that it?"

She stood up, walked around the dining-room table, then sat down on the other side. She had a fountain pen in her hand. "Now this," she said, pointing with the pen to another brochure, "this one is about New Mexico. I've never been to New Mexico. You haven't either, right?"

"No," Jeremy said. "Honey, what's this all about?"

"This," she said, "is all about what we're going to do during your two weeks off. I'll be damned if I'm going to sit here. Want to go to Santa Fe?"

Jeremy seemed itchy, as if he needed to go downstairs and play a few measures of jazz from Mars. "Sure, sure," he said. He rubbed his eyes suddenly. "Isn't it sort of hot that time of year?"

She shook her head. "It says here that the elevation's too high. You can stay in the mountains, and it's cool at night."

"Oh." Then, as an afterthought, he said, "Good."

She looked up at him. She stood and put her hand on his face, rubbing her thumb against his cheek. "How's the black box?" she asked. She had recently started to wear glasses and took them off now.

"How's the sky?" he asked. He turned around. "The black box is just fine. I move around it, but it's always there, right in front of me. It's hard to move with that damn thing in your head. I could write a book about it: how to live with a box and be a zombie." He reached for a beer and carried it to the basement. She could hear the television set being clicked on and the exhalation of the beer bottle when he opened it.

2

The flight to Albuquerque took four hours. Lunch was served halfway through: chicken in sauce. The stewardesses seemed proud of the meal and handed out the plastic trays with smug smiles. Jeremy had a copy of *Business Week* in his lap, which he dropped to the floor when the food arrived. For much of the four hours he sat back and dozed. Harriet was closer to the window and dutifully looked out whenever the captain announced that they were flying over a landmark.

In Albuquerque they rented a car and drove north toward Taos, the destination Harriet had decided upon, following the advice of the travel agent. They stopped at a Holiday Inn in

Santa Fe for dinner. Appalled by the congestion and traffic, they set out after breakfast the next morning. As they approached the mountains, Jeremy, who was driving, said, "So this is the broom that sweeps the cobwebs away." He said it softly and with enough irony to make Harriet wince and to pull at her eyebrow, a recent nervous tic. The trip, it was now understood, had been her idea. She was responsible. She offered him a stick of gum and turned on the radio. They listened to Willie Nelson and Charlie Daniels until the mountains began to interfere with the reception.

In Taos they drove through the city until they found the Best Western motel, pale-yellow and built in quasi-adobe style. They took showers and then strolled toward the center of town, holding hands. The light was brilliant and the air seemingly without the humidity and torpor of the midwest, but this atmosphere also had a kind of emptiness that Jeremy said he wasn't used to. In the vertical sun they could both feel their hair heating up. Harriet said she wanted a hat, and Jeremy nodded. He sniffed the air. They passed the Kit Carson museum, and Jeremy laughed to himself. "What is it?" Harriet asked, but he only shook his head. At the central square, the streets narrowed and the traffic backed up with motoring tourists. "Lots of art stores here," Harriet said, in a tone that suggested that Jeremy ought to be interested. She was gazing into a display window at a painting of what appeared to be a stick-figure man with a skull face dancing in a metallic, vulcanized landscape. She saw Jeremy's reflection in the window. He was peering at the stones on the sidewalk. Then she looked at herself: she was standing halfway in front of Jeremy, partially blocking his view.

They walked through the plaza, and Harriet went into a dime store to buy a hat. Jeremy sat outside on a bench in the square, opposite a hotel that advertised a display of the paintings of D. H. Lawrence, banned in England, so it was claimed.

He turned away. An old man, an Indian with shoulder-length gray hair, was crossing the plaza in front of him, murmuring an atonal chant. The tourists stepped aside to let the man pass. Jeremy glanced at the tree overhead, in whose shade he was sitting. He could not identify it. He exhaled and examined his Seiko angrily. He gazed down at the second hand circling the dial face once, then twice. He knew Harriet was approaching when he saw out of the corner of his eye her white cotton pants and her feet in their sandals.

"Do you like it?" she asked. He looked up. She had bought a yellow cap with a visor and the word "Taos" sewn into it. She was smiling, modeling for him.

"Very nice," he said. She sat down next to him and squeezed his arm. "What do people do in this town?" he asked. "Look at vapor trails all day?"

"They walk around," she said. "They buy things." She saw a couple dragging a protesting child into an art gallery. "They bully their kids." She paused, then went on, "They eat." She pointed to a restaurant, Casa Ogilvie's, on the east side of the square with a balcony that looked down at the commerce below. "Hungry?" He shrugged. "I sure am," she said. She took his hand and led him across the square into the archway underneath the restaurant. There she stopped, turned, and put her arms around him, leaning against him. She felt the sweat of his back against her palms. "I'm so sorry," she said. Then they went up the stairs and had lunch, two Margaritas each and enchiladas in hot sauce. Sweating and drowsy, they strolled back to the motel, not speaking.

They left the curtains of the front window open an inch or so when they made love that afternoon. From the bed they could see occasionally a thin strip of someone walking past. They made love to fill time, with an air of detachment, while the television set stayed on, showing a Lana Turner movie in which everyone's face was green at the edges and pink at the center. Jeremy and Harriet touched with the pleasure of being close to one familiar object in a setting crowded with strangers. Harriet reached her orgasm with her usual spasms of trembling, and when she cried out he lowered his head to the pillow on her right side, where he wouldn't see her face.

Thus began the pattern of the next three days: desultory shopping for knickknacks in the morning, followed by lunch, lovemaking and naps through the afternoon, during which time it usually rained for an hour or so. During their shopping trips they didn't buy very much: Jeremy said the art was mythic and lugubrious, and Harriet didn't like pottery. Jeremy bought a flashlight, in case, he said, the power went out, and Harriet purchased a keychain. All three days they went into Casa Ogilvie's at the same time and ordered the same meal, explaining to themselves that they didn't care to experiment with exotic regional food. On the third afternoon of this they woke up from their naps at about the same time with the totally clear unspoken understanding that they could not spend another day—or perhaps even another hour—in this manner.

Jeremy announced the problem by asking, "What do we do tomorrow?"

Harriet kicked her way out of bed and walked over to the television, on top of which she had placed a guide to the southwest. "Well," she said, opening it up, "there *are* sights around here. We haven't been into the mountains north of here. There's a Kiowa Indian Pueblo just a mile away. There's a place called Arroyo Seco near here and—"

"What's that?"

"It means Dry Gulch." She waited. "There's the Taos Gorge Bridge." Jeremy shook his head quickly. "The D. H. Lawrence shrine is thirty minutes from here, and so is the Millicent A. Rogers Memorial Museum. There are, it says here, some trout streams. If it were winter, we could go skiing."

"It's summer," Jeremy said, closing his eyes and pulling the sheet up. "We can't ski. What about this shrine?"

She put the book on the bed near Jeremy and read the entry. "It says that Lawrence lived for eighteen months up there, and they've preserved his ranch. When he died, they brought his ashes back and there's a shrine or something. They *call* it a shrine. I'm only telling you what the book says."

"D. H. Lawrence?" Jeremy asked sleepily.

"You know," Harriet said. *"Lady Chatterley's Lover."*

"Yes, I know." He smiled. "It wasn't the books I was asking about, it was the *quality* of the books, and therefore the necessity of making the trip."

"All I know is that it's visitable," she said, "and it's off State Highway Three, and it's something to do."

"Okay. I don't care what damn highway it's on," Jeremy said, reaching for the book and throwing it across the room. "Let's at least get into the car and go somewhere."

After breakfast they drove in the rented Pontiac out of town toward the Taos ski valley. They reached it after driving up fifteen miles of winding road through the mountains, following a stream of snow runoff, along which they counted a dozen fishermen. When they reached the valley, they admired the Sangre de Crísto Mountains but agreed it was summer and there was nothing to do in such a place. Neither blamed the other for acting upon an unproductive idea. They returned to the car and retraced their steps to the highway, which they followed for another fifteen miles until they reached the turn for the D. H. Lawrence shrine on the Kiowa Ranch Road. Jeremy stopped the car on the shoulder. "Well?" he asked.

"Why do we have to *decide* about everything?" Harriet said, looking straight ahead. "Why can't we just *do* it?"

He accelerated up the unpaved road, which climbed toward a plateau hidden in the mountains. They passed several farms where cattle were grazing on the thin grasses. The light made the land look varnished; even with sunglasses, Harriet squinted at the shimmering heat waves rising from the gravel.

Jeremy said, "What's here?"

"I told you. Anyhow, the description isn't much good. We'll find out. Maybe they'll have a tour of his inner sanctum or have his Nobel Prize up in a frame. The book says they have his actual typewriter."

Jeremy coughed. "He never won the Nobel Prize." Harriet looked over at him and noticed that his face was losing its internal structure and becoming puffy. Grief had added five years to his appearance. She saw, with disbelief, a new crease on his neck. Turning away, she glanced up at the sky: a hawk, cirrus clouds. The air conditioner was blowing a stream of cool air on her knees. Her gums ached.

"Only two more miles," Jeremy said, beginning now to hunch over the wheel slightly.

"I don't like this draft," she said, reaching over to snap off the air conditioner. She cranked down the window and let the breeze tangle her hair. They were still going uphill and had reached, a sign said, an elevation of nine thousand feet. Jeremy hummed Martian jazz as he drove, tapping the steering wheel. The little dirt road went past an open gate, divided in two, one fork going toward a conference center indicated by a road marker, the other toward the house and shrine. They came to a clearing. In front of them stood a two-story house looking a bit like an English country cottage, surrounded by a white picket fence, with a tire swing in the backyard, beyond which two horses were grazing. They were alone: there were no other cars in sight. Jeremy went up to the door of the house and knocked. A dog began barking angrily from inside, as if the knocks had interrupted its nap. "Look at this," Harriet said.

She had walked a few steps and was looking in the direction they had come from; in the clear air they could see down the mountain and across the valley for a distance of fifty miles or so. "It's beautiful," she said. Jeremy appeared from behind her, shielding his eyes although the sun was behind him. "What're you doing that for?" she asked.

"You have dark glasses. I don't."

"Where's the shrine?" she asked. "I don't see it anywhere."

"You have to turn around. Look." He pointed to the picket fence. At its north corner there was a sign that Harriet had missed.

SHRINE ☛

"That's very quaint," she said. "And what's this?" She walked toward the fence and picked a child's mitten off one of the posts. Mickey Mouse's face was printed on the front of the mitten, and one of his arms reached up over the thumb. She began laughing. "It doesn't say anything about Mickey Mouse in *Fodor's*. Do you think he's part of the shrine?"

Jeremy didn't answer. He had already started out ahead of her on a path indicated by the black pointing finger. Harriet followed him, panting from the altitude and the blistering heat, feeling her back begin to sweat as the light rained down on it. She felt the light on her legs and inside her head, on her eardrums. The path turned to the right and began a series of narrowing zigzags going up the side of a hill at the top of which stood the shrine, a small white boxlike building that, as they approached it, resembled a chapel, a mausoleum, or both. A granite phoenix glowered at the apex of the roof.

"The door's open," Jeremy said, twenty feet ahead of her, "and nobody's here." He was wearing heavy jeans, and his blue shirt was soaked with two wings of sweat. Harriet could hear the rhythmic pant of his breathing.

"Are there snakes out here?" she asked. "I hate snakes."

"Not in the shrine," he said. "I don't see any."

"What do you see?"

"A visitors' register." He had reached the door and had stepped inside. Then he came back out.

She was still ten feet away. "There must be more. You can't have a shrine without something in it."

"Well, there's this white thing outside," he said breathlessly. "Looks like a burial stone." She was now standing next to him. "Yes. This is where his wife is buried." They both looked at it. A small picture of Frieda was bolted into the stone.

"Well," Jeremy said, "now for the shrine." They shuffled inside. At the back was a small stained-glass window, a representation of the sun, thick literalized rays burning out from its center. To their left the visitors' register lay open on a high desk, and above it in a display case three graying documents asserted that the ashes stored here were authentically those of D. H. Lawrence, the author. The chapel's interior smelled of sage and cement. At the far side of the shrine, six feet away, was a roped-off area, and at the back an approximation of an altar, at whose base was a granite block with the letters DHL carved on it. "This is it?" Jeremy asked. "No wonder no one's here."

Harriet felt giddy from the altitude. "Should we pray?" she asked, but before Jeremy could answer, she said, "Well, good for him. He got himself a fine shrine. Maybe he deserves it. Goddamn, it's hot in here." She turned around and walked outside, still laughing in a broken series of almost inaudible chuckles. When she was back in the sun, she pointed her finger the way the sign had indicated and said, "Shrine."

Jeremy stepped close to her, and they both looked again at the mountains in the west. "I used to read him in college," Harriet said, "and in high school I had a copy of *The Rainbow* I hid under my pillow where my mother wouldn't find it. Jesus, it must be ninety-five degrees." She looked suddenly at Jeremy, sweat dripping into her eyes. "I used to have a lot of fantasies when I was a teenager," she said. He was wiping his face with a handkerchief. "Do you see anyone?" she asked.

"Do I see anybody? No. We would've heard a car coming up the road. Why?"

"Because I'm hot. I feel like doing something," Harriet

said. "I mean, here we are at the D. H. Lawrence shrine." She was unbuttoning her blouse. "I just thought of this," she said, beginning to laugh again. She put her blouse on the ground and quickly unhooked her bra, dropping it on top of the blouse. "There," she said, sighing. "Now that's better." She turned to face the mountains. When Jeremy didn't say anything, she swung around to look at him. He was staring at her, at the brown circles of her nipples, and his face seemed stricken. She reached over and took his hand. "Oh, Jay, sweetie," she said, "no one will see us. Honey. What is it? Do you want me to get dressed?"

"That's not it." He was staring at her, as if she were not his wife.

"What? What is it?"

"You're free of it." He wiped his forehead.

"What?"

"You're free of it. You're leaving me alone here."

"Alone? Alone in what?"

"You know perfectly damn well," he said. "I'm alone back here." He tapped his head. "I don't know how you did it, but you did it. You broke free. You're gone." He bent down. "You don't know what I'm talking about."

"Yes, I do." She put her bra and blouse back on and turned toward him again. His face was a mixture of agony and rage, but in the huge sunlight these emotions diminished to small vestigial puffs of feeling. "It's a path," she said. "And then you're surprised. You get out. It'll happen to you. You'll see. Honestly."

She could see his legs shaking. His face was a barren but expressive landscape. "Okay," he said. "Talk all you want. I was just thinking . . . " He didn't finish the sentence.

"You'll be all right," she said, stroking his back.

"I don't *want* to be all right!" he said, his voice rising, a horrible smile appearing on his face: it was a devil's face, Harriet saw, and it was radiant and calm. Sweat poured off his forehead, and his skin had started to flush pink. "It's my plea-sure not to be all right. Do you see that? My *pleasure*."

She wiped her hands on her cotton pants. A stain appeared, then vanished. "You want that? You want to be back there by yourself?"

"Yeah." He nodded. "You bet. I feel like an explorer. I feel like a fucking pioneer." He gave each one of the words a sepa-rate emphasis. Meanwhile, he had separated himself from her and was now tilting his head up toward the sky, letting the sun shine on his closed eyelids.

She looked at him. In the midst of the sunlight he was hug-ging his darkness. She stepped down the zigzag path to the car leaving him there, but he followed her. Once they were both in the car, the dog inside the ranch house began its frantic bark-ing, but it stopped after a few seconds. She took Jeremy's hand and scanned the clouds in the west, the Sangre de Crísto Mountains to the east, trying to see the sky, the beckoning clouds, the way he did, but she couldn't. All she could see was the land stretched out in front of her, and, far in the distance, all fifty miles away, a few thunderheads and a narrow curtain of rain, so thin that the light passed straight through it.

Talk Show

✦

Clutching a stuffed green dragon in one hand, the boy stands patiently at the Thermopane window, gazing out at the snowy fenced backyard where the birds flutter down to the feeder, which hangs on a copper wire from a branch of the apple tree. In his other hand the boy holds a microphone disconnected from a tape recorder, its lead wire dangling on the floor. The wind, from Canada, blows the feeder so that it swings roughly back and forth. The boy is just five; he is whispering into the microphone. "Calling the birds. At noon the TV weatherman said colder weather is on the way, and more snow, and some blue sky, but it's secret, don't tell, be careful, shhh . . ." As he watches, a male cardinal and a nuthatch fly suddenly straight up, as if startled.

Darth Vader and Gort the robot, part of a packet of Hanukkah presents by mail from the boy's two Jewish relatives who live in Denver, stand on the Chutes and Ladders board. Gort, who wears a helmet, is ten spaces ahead of Darth. Darth has fallen down several long curving chutes that Gort has missed. The boy has never seen *Star Wars* and does not know Darth's mythology; for him, Darth is a pathetic character, a loser. He picks him up and pats him on the head. "It's all right," he says, putting him back on the board on the wrong square. "Maybe you'll catch up." The boy hiccups and presses his finger to his lips, dry and chapped from forced-air heating.

Now the boy, whose name is Louie, is looking at a picture book. Called *Animals of Africa*, it is an oversized glossy volume from the public library containing many four-color illustrations. Louie is lying on his stomach in his room turning its pages and talking into the microphone. Looking at four giraffes eating the leaves of acacia and mimosa trees, he says, "Christmas is over. I got everything I asked for." He turns to a page showing sleepy lions. "Yesterday I ate some Pepperidge Farm cookies." A hyena: "I'm going to nursery school in an hour." A herd of antelope: "If I fell too far out of a tree I would die and be dead." Rufus, the dog, comes over to lick him on the face, hoping for some action.

Louie's father invented the talk show. Coming home late in the afternoon, his father takes off his coat and sits down in the La-Z-Boy. Louie comes over to him with the microphone. "And now, heeeeere's Daddy," Louie says. His father takes the microphone and says, "This is the talk show for today. Well, this morning I got into my car and drove to work. It was a nice morning. I liked the sun. Then I had lunch, which was sandwiches and tea. Then I had my afternoon work and then I was so tired I had to come home. And now . . . over to Louie!" The boy takes the microphone. "Well, folks, today I played with my trains. Mommy took me to a store to buy a cap." Louie waits, remembering. "The one I got is blue. It has earmuffs. I saw *Sesame Street*. I guess that's all for today."

When he draws on his blackboard, attached by his mother to a closet door in the basement, he uses green chalk for straight lines and red chalk for circles. He draws the circles first, then draws the green lines through them. "Here come the space invaders," he says. When the green lines pierce the circles, the boy says, "Ouch. Don't do that. Ow. Stop." When he is finished and the chalkboard is covered with scattered lines, he says, "All the lines learned how to cooperate and lived happily ever after in lineland, where they were sort of friends."

———

Playing on the enclosed porch with his Lego blocks, the boy looks out the window at the backyard and for a moment imagines himself playing in the sandbox in the middle of winter. The sandbox is twenty feet away from the apple tree and the bird feeder, but it is invisible under all this Michigan snow. He reaches behind some blocks for his microphone. "Well," he says, "maybe there's a kid out there playing in the snow. Nobody knows what he is doing out there. Will he stay out? Will he come in? Nobody knows. Goodbye." He covers his eyes and shakes his head, in a fit of giggling.

Louie is an only child. Much of the day is occupied with his private projects. He gets into arguments with his stuffed animals. He says, "The magician changed the fieldmice into green turtles and poison purple fruit trees," and one of his animals, the platypus puppet, shakes its head. "No. Yes. No. Yes. No. Yes," the boy says.

The branches of the apple tree are not moving now; the day is cloudy; snow rests heavily on the branches of the tree and the boy's jungle gym. Behind the house nothing moves except for water dripping down from the icicles suspended from the gutter, and the water drips only in the midafternoon, when the sun is out.

On rare clear nights, the moon has a bright silver radiance, rising like an electric dime over the house across the street and then hanging precariously over the streetlight outside of Louie's window. Then the moon goes a little crazy, pours light over Louie's face, scatters light everywhere, a steady stream of moonlight flows into the room, the light makes his bed shiver, rise, drown. Sometimes, pulling himself with difficulty out of his dreams, as he looks out of his bedroom window, awake in the middle of the night, Louie begins to hiccup, and the streetlight goes out, just like that: first light, hiccup, then dark. Louie watches the moon and thinks of waking his mother. The moon stays on.

Louie's mother gets calls after lunch. The calls are from Hawaii, where her parents are wintering. Louie's grandmother has become very sick. Louie's mother stands in the kitchen listening to the telephone, while Louie plays on the porch, pushing his train across the switch track.

In the backyard the birds perch on the telephone lines, their feathers puffed out against the cold. The biggest birds, the doves, are the least active. They are poor observers, unlike the chickadees, and are interested in nothing to either the right or left. The chickadees hop from the swing set to the telephone wires to the bird feeder and then fly back to the forest. The nuthatches are more shy than the chickadees and move their heads with nervous flicks. Louie watches them stop on the phone lines. Do they hear voices through their feet?

Louie snaps off Mr. Rogers. "You don't live in *my* neighborhood," he says.

The boy has seen *The Day the Earth Stood Still* many times on television. It is his favorite movie. His father has videotaped it. In it, the visitor from outer space, Klaatu, stops all electricity on earth for thirty minutes. He does this to get earthlings to pay attention to his message, which is that earthlings with their passion for warfare are endangering the rest of the universe. Klaatu's enforcer is the robot, Gort. Gort zaps guns and tanks. The moment in the film that the boy always talks about occurs when Klaatu, whose earth name is Mr. Carpenter, is shot and killed by the army but then revived on his spaceship by a noisy shrieking machine. After seeing the movie after dinner on the VCR, Louie runs upstairs. The streetlight is back on.

"Here is the talk show for today," the boy says, imitating Guy Smiley's emcee voice on *Sesame Street*. "So so so so. Grandma's in the hospital in Hawaii. Mommy's feeling pretty miserable." He holds the microphone closer to his mouth for an effect of immediacy. "Will Grandma get better? Worse? Nobody knows!" It sounds like the announcement of a prize. "And now, over to Daddy." And he hands the microphone to his father.

Unannounced, his Aunt Laurel comes for a visit, and it has something to do with the crisis in Hawaii. Aunt Laurel: with her curly brown hair that surrounds her head like a soft cushion in case she should collide with anything, and her thick-soled running shoes. She sleeps on the sofa in the living room, her radio next to her on the floor, and her Walkman under the pillow in case she wakes up and needs music immediately. She gives Louie a present: a one-dollar bill embedded forever inside a cube of clear Lucite. Louie puts it in the drawer with his underwear. Aunt Laurel makes hundreds of chocolate cookies during the two days she visits, using up all the butter. Her perfume, L'Air du Temps, precedes her and follows her around the house like a primal announcement. Louie thinks he can taste L'Air du Temps in her cookies. And then, as suddenly as she came, she is gone.

In bed he counts his fingers. His parents are not awake. Somehow it comes out to eleven. He tries again. Ten this time. Once more. And again the sum comes out to eleven. He holds his hands up in the semidark, silhouetting them against his Swiss-chalet nightlight. He twists his hands to the right and left. He curls and uncurls his fingers. Where is the extra finger? He counts again: ten. He closes his eyes and tries to go back to sleep, sighing.

Laurel, who is Mommy's sister, doesn't have any kids. But Mommy's other sister, Beth, has two: Henry and Annie, Louie's cousins, half brother and sister because Beth has been married twice, first to Uncle Douglas, a plumber in Grand Rapids, and then to Uncle Reeve, the computer software salesman in Cincinnati. Daddy has one brother, Uncle Newton, who works in the Pentagon and is married to Aunt Sarah. Then there is Daddy's other brother, Uncle Bardwell, who is a big secret and has never been seen. Nobody ever mentions him. You can't even always call him Uncle Bardwell. "Don't call him that!" "Why not?" "Just don't." And of course there is Mr. Fleisch, who is sort of made-up.

What is happening to Grandma? At night the January winds blow against the house, bending it, making it creak. "It's the joints creaking," his mother says. What joints? "The joints in the house." Where are they? "They're in the walls." What do they do? "They let the house move when it's cold and windy." Why does it have to move? "I don't know. Go to sleep."

The lights won't quite go off in the dining room, the lights attached to the ceiling chandelier, the lights with clear glass tapered bulbs. When Louie walks downstairs in the dark, wearing his green pajamas and size five Grinnell College sweatshirt, the lights glow and flicker. There is moisture inside the walls, his father has said. This moisture creates short circuits in the old wiring and the short circuits keep the electricity, which his father calls "juice," going to the bulbs when it shouldn't. Mr. O'Donnelly will come soon to fix it. Louie looks at the lights, switched off, but flickering with thin orange pulsations. The light is so dim he can see the filaments perfectly outlined in the bulbs. He doesn't want these lights to be on, not when they're supposed to be off, not at all, not even a little bit. He pads back up the stairs.

"This is the talk show," he whispers into his microphone, lying in his bed in the middle of the night. "Everybody's sleeping. It's cold out. My dragon is here. Outside . . . " He gets up and pokes his head under the window shade. "Outside the moon is on, but the streetlight is off. And that's all for today."

His face on the underside of a spoon is a pumpkin face. On the opposite side of the spoon it's upside down, thin as a scarecrow, except close up. Then it's all lips.

A clear sunny January morning. He is out on his Champion F-47 sled, going down a hill two blocks from the house. His father watches him. Louie rides down the hill, trots up dragging the sled, rides down again. His face glows and he sings loudly to himself.

Who is Mr. Fleisch? Louie's father admits in public that the idea was a bad one. Because Louie would not go to bed one night, Louie's father said, "Mr. Fleisch will come get you. He gets all bad boys who won't go to bed. He steals them and puts them in his dirty brown bag. No one ever sees those boys again." Louie was terrified. Now he wants to know more about Mr. Fleisch. Louie's father says there is no Mr. Fleisch, but Louie says there is. Louie knows because he has heard his parents arguing about Mr. Fleisch. He heard his mother say, "You should never have talked about him in front of Mr. Big Ears. You should never have started this."

When he thinks about his grandmother, he thinks about how she said, "Hi, Louie!" and hugged him and kissed him and gave him cookies, and how she and Grandfather live on the fourth floor of a building with a doorman. He remembers how she took him downtown and let him ride the elevators. She had a leopard-skin rug at the foot of her bed, and like Aunt Laurel she sometimes wore powerful perfume. When he thinks about how she might die, he doesn't believe it, and he wants teeth as big as the leopard's.

Louie squints. Dazzling sunlight. Blue sky, sun on snow. Louie is in his snowsuit, complete with leggings. His winter coat so tight that his arms want to stick straight out. He is in his playmate Patrick's backyard building a fort, which turns into a snowman. Now they jump on the snowman and roll around in the snow, screaming and giggling. Louie wrestles with Patrick. When Patrick's mother tells them to come in, they both shout "No!" together, a team of two boys against one mother.

The puffed red cardinal sits on the perch of the bird feeder, holding on. The sunny wind blows the feeder back and forth. Louie knocks on the window, but the bird does not scare.

Louie's mother is on the phone all the time. She is talking about airplanes and hospitals, and Louie's grandmother. Then she is packing. It is all arranged. They will go see her.

Gort the robot and Darth Vader are having a fight. Louie pushes the two figures together and says, "Urrrrrr. Boom bang." He hits one plastic character with the other. Suddenly, unexpectedly, the silvery arm of Gort falls right off, detached at the shoulder. Louie puts the two figures down on the kitchen counter and walks into the living room, where he turns on the TV.

In nursery school he presses a toy button, just lying there in the toy box, attached to nothing. When he does, Sylvia, across the room, near the window, screams. He pushes the button again and again Sylvia screams. He runs over to Sylvia and asks her why she screamed. She says, "'Cause I felt like it."

Now he is on the airplane, flying to Hawaii. He has his dragon, and his microphone, and his coloring books, and C3PO, and Darth Vader, and his Paddington books, and two Duplo blocks to open and close as elevator doors. He looks past his mother's window seat first at the Grand Canyon and then at the ocean. He sleeps and watches a movie for grown-ups. He goes to the bathroom a lot. His father sits on the aisle seat, staring straight ahead.

In Hawaii the birds are different. The cardinals are red only at the backs of their heads. The rest of their bodies are gray. Many of the other birds are yellow, like the canaries sold at the back of Woolworth's. Nobody wears snowsuits. There is traffic jammed around Queen's Hospital. In the hotel, Louie's room is on the ninth floor. The sun never goes out, and people stroll on the beach in front of the hotel. In the hospital lobby Louie plays with the water fountain and watches the elevator doors while his mother is upstairs. He and his father go into the gift shop and look at pocket mirrors and tiny flashlights that can be attached to books, for reading in bed.

The sand on the beach is bright, and the sun burns off the water, and the intensity makes Louie squint. Holding his father's hand, Louie chases a crab down a stone breakwater. Then the crab hides inside a stone pocket. Now Louie is making a sand castle. Tourists walk restlessly in front and in back of him on the beach. Young men with two-day beards crawl out of their sleeping bags, stretch, and read their books. A fat man with red inflated cheeks and a stomach that hangs over the front of his swimming suit appears. The man has a cigar in his mouth, a small white dog on a leash in one hand, and a cane in the other. Louie has never seen a cane on the beach. He looks away. The dog tries to pee on Louie's sand castle, but the man gives its leash a yank, and they both walk on.

He is hopping on the balcony of someone who is baby-sitting for him, someone known only as Jane. Here the balconies are called lanais. Jane's house is in a building and is eight floors up. Everyone here lives far above the ground. The lanai does not shake when Louie jumps on it. It is less a balcony than a windy shelf. On it he plays. He pushes one of his cars to the edge and it falls off. Louie can see it tumble down end over end. He and Jane go down to the parking lot to get it. It's not broken. It works fine.

The live characters on *Sesame Street* include Bob, the Irish tenor; Gordon and Susan, Big Bird's surrogate parents; Maria, who fixes radios; Luis, who has the lowest voice; David, a slightly excitable guy who runs Mr. Hooper's store; Olivia, who has the best voice and who is the sweetest; Lynda, who is deaf and works in a library; and Mr. Hooper, who died at Thanksgiving and gave his store to David. David has learned how to make Big Bird's birdseed sundaes, but it is not the same as when Mr. Hooper made them. In Hawaii, they get *Sesame Street*, same as on the mainland. Louie yells and throws things if the trips to the hospital and the beach force him to miss it.

The fat man who walks on the beach with a cane is there every day, exercising his dog, a white terrier suffering from eczema. The terrier barks at everybody, including Louie. Sometimes the waves rush in and get its paws wet. Then the terrier barks irritably at the ocean. Every inch of the fat man's body is oiled and brown. He looks like an ad for a tanning lotion, except for his huge size and blubbery shape.

———

Louie has the microphone in the car. "We won't be making any more trips to the hospital today. I won't tell you folks out there why 'cause it's a little too miserable."

Menus that he cannot read descend in front of his face for breakfast, lunch, and dinner. Waiters bring glasses of water filled to the brim with ice, and the ice always falls into his lap. In one restaurant, called T. G. I. Friday's, the bathroom is lit with red spotlights and has a red neon sign above the urinal that his father says spells BANK. No matter what restaurant they go to, Louie gets hamburger and french fries. That's all he wants, and it's all he'll eat.

In Honolulu the streetlights do not blink, as they do on Louie's street at home. They're on all night, steadily. Another one of his baby-sitters, Mrs. Yamashita, takes him to a park near the aquarium and shows him the lizards. "They don't bite," she says. "They eat flies." Mrs. Yamashita lives on the fourteenth floor of her building. Louie wants to know where the thirteenth floor is. "No thirteenth floor," Mrs. Yamashita says. "Never thirteenth floor. Bad luck." "For grown-ups?" Louie asks. Mrs. Yamashita shrugs. "What floor comes after twelve?" "Fourteen. Always fourteenth floor. You are some boy for questions."

His nightmare: a monster comes and rips all his skin off.

In some of the restaurants, the ones on verandas and covered terraces, the birds fly in and flutter around at his feet. He drops small pellets of bread for them that he has torn off his roll. What kinds of birds are they? House sparrows. "No," his father says. "Swallowtails. Waxwings. Flycatchers. Thrush. Red-headed—" "Stop it," his mother says. "We're *all* under a strain."

———

Before bed his mother puts the bedtime music on and holds him in her lap, and he builds small sentences with short wooden block words about his fears and what he thinks is happening. As long as she holds him and tells him it's all right, it *is* all right, but then she has to tuck him in and give him up to the erratic care and passions of sleep.

What does she look like? She has a tube up her nose. She can't talk. She isn't sleeping. She thrashes back and forth on the bed. Her throat fills with sputum. They give her suction with a plastic hose that snakes down her throat. She looks scared. They have disconnected her from the machines. It's no problem for Louie to overhear any of this.

They have flowers here with red waxy petals, and ground cover in the residential areas fed by buried sprinkler pipe, and trees with subdivided trunks held up by broomstick roots. Some branches hang down like shredded snakeskin. The grass doesn't exactly look like grass: more like healthy organic silk. Near the reefs the water's color is deep blue, and just outside the city the palm trees drop coconuts near a playpark. Louie watches the local kids throw the coconuts against the slide and the teeter-totter, and eventually the coconuts crack apart, leaving milk splattered on the aluminum in patterns which, when they dry, look like white cobwebs.

At last he has the courage to ask. "Are you Mr. Fleisch?" The man stops, leans on his cane, and through his dark glasses looks at Louie's sand harbor. "Why, no," he says. "I'm Dr. deVries. Do we know each other?" Louie shakes his head. The terrier barks at Louie and at the waves.

Beyond the reef the Pacific Ocean reflects laterally the silver of the clouds that hang over it, the clouds that, when they reach the land, drop rain faster than Louie has ever seen it fall, like rain *thrown* frighteningly to the ground and into the garden of the house of his grandfather's friend, where they happen to be visiting right now, when Louie's mother arrives by taxi from the hospital, and takes Louie in her arms. Rain falls into the empty swimming pool, and the wind and surf roar more loudly, and someone tells Louie not to go outside; he might be hit by a falling coconut. As the storm increases in intensity, his mother begins to tell him a story about a rabbit, but he falls asleep long before the story is over.

Once when he was lying sleepy under the covers, humming syllables of a song he had made up himself, he looked toward his toy shelf. At that moment a police car with dead batteries drove off the shelf and landed on the floor, its wheels still turning, as if it had been pushed.

Just after dinner, back in the hotel, he picks up the microphone. "This is the talk show for today. How is Grandma? She's not worse, she's not better, she's dead." He puts the microphone down and goes into the bedroom to play with his Lego blocks. He watches the windows carefully.

Louie says he'll scream if he has to go to the funeral. His mother says he doesn't have to.

On the airplane home he sets up Darth Vader and Gort the robot on the tray table. Darth kills Gort. Then Darth kills Gort's car. Then he kills Gort's feet. Then he kills Gort's train and his toothbrush and his swimming pool. Then Gort gets up and kisses Darth and says it's really okay. The stewardess leans down and smiles. Who's this? she asks. Darth Vader? Yah, Louie says. Zap! He aims the weapon in Darth's hand at her. Am I dead? the stewardess asks, smiling. Zap, Louie says. Zap zap zap. His mother and father both tell him to stop it.

The snow in the backyard is deeper by about six inches than it was before he left. Wearing his insulated mittens and his thermal jacket, Louie sinks his arm down into the snow. His father is filling the tube with birdseed. Can I make a snow angel? Louie asks. Sure, his father says. Why not. But he doesn't lie down. He just stands there, looking out at the woods.

They are sitting at the front window of Mr. Steak. His father is asking him if he knows where the street in front of the restaurant goes. Sure, Louie says, pointing to the left. That way's hither. Then he points to the right. And that way's yon.

Is anyone going to call Uncle Bardwell? No. No one *ever* calls Uncle Bardwell. He's in the other family, and besides, no one knows where he is. How can an uncle disappear? He just can.

The monster has three green eyes and a cigar and a chain vest and its feet are on backwards. It picks Louie up and throws him down on a cobbled sidewalk and then scrubs his skin off with SOS pads. Its fingernails are as long as new copper pennies and as shiny. The monster's mouth forms the perfect circle of an open tin can. His voice sounds like an accordion played down at the end of a tunnel. The sentences he says are terrible and scary. Now the monster is chasing Louie down the woods, into the crowded street, out onto the lanai. It picks Louie up and throws him down ten floors until Louie breaks. Oh, Louie shouts in his sleep. Oh, oh.

The dog, Rufus, home at last from the kennel where he was being boarded, races into the house from the car through the kitchen door, slips on the Solarian, falls near the refrigerator, skids his claws across the surface, leaving scratch marks, gets to his feet, and runs into the living room, where Louie is sitting in a patch of sun near the window, building a hotel made out of cardboard bricks. Rufus knocks over the bricks with his tail and bounds into Louie's lap, covering him with kisses and slobber. He barks once. Then he runs back into the kitchen, searching for food.

At midday in the winter, the sparrows perch at the chimney top next to the furnace vent, staying warm in the heat expelled from the house into the air. Louie can see the birds on the neighbor's chimney: seven of them crowded together on the masonry.

In nursery school his classmates gather around him to look at his tan and to hear about coconuts. Louie sits down on the floor next to a Playmobile spaceship and tells Caroline and DJ about the sunshine, palm trees, and his grandmother in the hospital bed, whom he did not actually see but did hear about. His teacher overhears this and asks if there was a funeral. Yes, Louie says, but *I* didn't go.

Louie sits in the backseat of his mother's car, which is accelerating down the freeway toward the Warehouse Foods outlet. Then they are pulled over by a police car, whose flashing red light Louie can just see when he twists around and looks out through the back window from his Safe-T-Seat. The officer, a man wearing the largest dark glasses Louie has ever seen, comes to his mother's side of the car and gives her a ticket for speeding. Louie's mother does a lot of nodding and agreeing with the policeman. When she has taken the ticket and is driving on the freeway again, she begins wiping her eyes.

"Today," Louie says into the microphone, "we were arrested on the freeway. Mommy started to cry. We went to a food store where they had magic doors that opened when you just stood in front of them. I played in the snow when we got home. I saw *Sesame Street* just before nursery school. I guess that's all for today. Over to Daddy." He hands the microphone to his father, who says, "Sorry, Louie. No news is good news." He gives the microphone back.

When the snow falls in what the weathermen call "snow showers," each flake seems to have its own body of space around it. Each flake falls slowly, buoyed by the cold dense air, in the calm of January.

Louie is looking out through the Thermopane glass into the backyard, where snow is falling and the sparrows have assembled in the apple tree, twenty sparrows at least, crowded together in the upper branches. Louie stares at them. When he says, "Grandma," all the birds fly straight up, and then Louie sees that it is not his word that has startled them, but the dog, Rufus, who has just run out from the garage and who now makes zigzag turns, sudden starts, and leaps underneath the bird feeder, growling and snapping at the sky.

Cataract

✦

At the dinner table Walter Lundholm, Sr., toys with the silver pepper shaker, wondering how to announce his plans for an early retirement to his wife. They have both been eating overcooked beef burgundy, and now Jane is relating an anecdote about what happened at the A&P this afternoon. It seems that a rather shabby-looking man with a broad, piggish face fell down in a dead faint in front of the meat counter and had to be revived by two grocery boys. While Jane is telling this story, the sound of rhythmic clapping leaks out from the kitchen, where the Lundholms' cook, Vernice, is listening to Pentecostal radio while she does the dishes.

Walter is following Jane's story, but he is looking at the fleur-de-lis pattern wallpaper. Every thirty seconds, he nods. What he wants to say to his wife is that they don't need more money and he wants to stop earning it. In worldly terms, this is not a large problem, but it happens to be associated in his mind with the unpleasant aching glow he has lately felt radiating out of his chest. What he does not want to say to Jane is that if he works much longer at developing real estate properties along high-intensity freeways, he too will eventually fall to the floor in supermarkets. He listens as she concludes her story, with the piggish man coming to, and walking home by himself.

"And with no groceries," Jane says. "Imagine. What do you suppose he was doing there?" She waits. "Walter, why are you playing with that pepper shaker? You've finished your meal."

"I've been thinking."

"What? What have you been thinking about?"

"Giving up the office." He watches her reaction. "I'm going

to let Gordon and Kenny buy me out. They've made offers. I'm tired of the business. I've been meaning to tell you."

"Well," she says, reaching for the string of pearls around her neck. "My goodness. This is quite a surprise. You're not being silly, are you? This isn't one of your moods? You *do* get obsessive about things."

"No." He is gazing at the pearls. "It's not a mood. I've thought about it for months."

"Months. Well, this is the first *I've* heard. What will you do?" She has a sip of wine. "Start a new business?"

"No. Not that. No more money. I want to try something different." He smiles and looks directly at her. "I want to paint again."

"Paint?" She clasps her hands together. *"Paint?* Walter, dear, you haven't painted since your college days. Why on earth did you think of that? *What* do you want to paint?"

He folds his napkin. "Well, landscapes, to start with. I have this idea about a barn." He draws a barn in the air. "An image. I think about it quite often. I've even dreamt about it." From the living-room FM stereo comes the sound of dinner music, the Brahms Clarinet Quintet. He arranges his fork and knife on the plate. "I want to drive out to the countryside and paint whatever I see."

"Well." She tilts her head back. "I am trying to take all of this evenly and calmly. Believe me, it's not easy." She touches her hair. "I don't know *what* our friends will say. I suppose we shall make some accommodations. I can't say I was prepared for this piece of news, but I will do my best. Do you think you'll be able to fill all the hours of the day with this new hobby of yours?"

"I don't know."

"I don't know either. We'll see." She gives him a social smile. "I imagine it'll be good for your blood pressure. One hundred sixty-five over ninety is no joke." She looks as if she is adding numbers. Apparently the results of these calculations do not cause her excessive distress, because she picks up her wineglass and looks out the bay window toward the driveway. "Painting," she says. "Now whatever put that into your mind? Whom were you thinking of? Rembrandt? Degas?"

He looks down at his plate. "No. Not them."

"Well, then. Who inspired you?"

"Winston Churchill," he says. "I want to paint like that."

Now, a month later, Walter's canvas, easel, floppy hat, chair, and oils are loaded up in the back of his Buick Electra, and he is driving out from suburban Minneapolis along Highway 7 into rural Minnesota, looking for a scene to paint. He wants a barn. A barn stands in the right-hand background of his imagination, with the rest of the canvas filled with fields and sky. Many barns have been torn down to make way for Walter's development properties, and now, in his own small way, he wants to save one. He thinks of the barn as reddish-brown but has not decided what color the fields should be.

In central Minnesota Walter finds himself off the freeway and the state highway he meant to follow. He is speeding down a dirt road at forty-five miles an hour. His car throws up a turbulent wake of light brown dust. Where is the right barn? Most of them are marred geometrically by deep-blue Harvestore silos that put them in shadow. What Walter wants is an individual barn, by itself, a proud symbol of something or other.

Ahead and to his right he sees a barn and decides that, yes, this one will have to do. Red, with the proper slanted rooflines, and a wide door at its loft with hinges at the top, it shows some age in its mottled texture, as if it needed carpentry work and two coats of paint. Slit windows look out from the loft on the north side. A weather vane perches at the center, a blue glass bulb in its stalk.

What is the etiquette of painting a stranger's field and barn? Permission is required. Farming is not a business for tourists.

He drives off the dirt road and up the driveway, stopping fifty feet from the house. This house is white, and, more important, it *looks* like a farmhouse; it even has four lightning rods at its cardinal points. The yard itself has a rose arbor ten feet away from a clothesline, on which hang two yellow bath towels and two white bedsheets. A black cat is asleep underneath one of the sheets. Everything looks exactly the way it's supposed to. To his left stand a rickety shed and a doghouse with broken shingles, but no dog in view. A broken toy windmill flaps far back in the yard. And then there are the fields, passive and flat, stretching far away, holding their seedling crops he cannot identify.

Careful to leave his sunhat in the car, he knocks at the door; he does not ring the doorbell. At a farmhouse, a knock is more appropriate, more in the spirit of things. After waiting a moment, he is greeted by a slender boy, ten or eleven years old, wearing orthopedic shoes and thin wire glasses.

"Yeah?" he says, looking down at Walter, who stands on the bottom step. "Do I know you?"

"No," Walter says. "We haven't met."

The boy swallows. "You want something?"

"I'm a painter. I want to paint a picture of your barn. From the road, so I can get the fields in it, too."

"Is that all?" the boy asks. "You're a painter? You're asking if you can paint our place?" He shrugs. "Suit yourself, mister."

"If you want me to do something," Walter says, "I will."

"Huh?" The boy turns on the porch and looks at him. "Do what? You aren't a doctor or something, are you?"

"What? No, I'm not." He waits. "I'll pay you if you want."

"Mister," the boy says, "we're busy here, okay? I've got things I got to do. Go ahead and paint your picture."

"Thanks," Walter says, backing through the yard to his car. He smells compost, as he opens the door and turns on the radio to static. He parks off the country road, making sure that the car is almost in the ditch, out of everyone's way.

An hour later, with his easel set up, Walter feels the sun at his back, front-lighting the barn so that it appears to have a brilliant uncompromised visual integrity. Protected by his hat, his canvas in front of him, his oils ready, he is ready to paint what he sees. The only trouble is that he feels awful. His chest is glowing and aching, and he feels displaced, the one thing that is visually wrong in this landscape where everything else is right.

As he paints, a portly man in a gray Oldsmobile arrives at the farmhouse and carries a leather bag inside. Yes, this *would* be the doctor. Thirty minutes later the same man leaves, waving at the boy, who stands inside the screen door sucking an orange popsicle. The boy glances at Walter and goes back inside. The doctor slows down to look at Walter's painting, opens the window and shouts, "Not bad!" and then spins his tires on the dirt road. By now Walter has drawn the outlines of a barn, and he has the mix of colors right, ready for the painting-in. His throat is itching.

Now another car turns into the farm's driveway, a blue two-door Ford. Will this parade of cars ever stop? A woman wearing jeans and a pale-pink blouse gets out, followed by a black Labrador dog. She crosses the lawn and steps up to the porch. Walter, working on the horizon line across the top third of the canvas, glances at the farmhouse, not in the painting but the one in his line of sight, and there at the window on the second floor is a man's face, probably the boy's father, looking straight out at him, pale and accusatory.

Walter adjusts his easel, hiding behind it for a moment. His back aches, and his throat feels dusty. He paints quickly, hoping that if he skips lunch he can finish enough of the picture to complete it at home. His image of Churchill, smoking Havana cigars and sitting on the cliffs at Cornwall while he paints the immense apolitical ocean, doesn't correspond to what he is experiencing now, in this claustrophobic field. Twice he catches himself painting with his eyes on the farmhouse where the man stares down on him, and for a moment Walter thinks of the way animals look out from behind bars in the zoo.

Insects are making their crazed noises behind Walter, and gnats cluster over his head, tiny dots of leaping aggressive life flying into his ears and hair. In the painting, the barn stands placid and self-contained, settled to the ground, mixed and concentrated by proportioned midwestern sky. Walter pours himself Lipton tea from a thermos into a red plastic cup. There is that man. *What does he want?* Late in the afternoon, Walter packs up and leaves, giving one last glance at the emptied upstairs bedroom window.

When he walks into the house at six-thirty, Jane examines him with genteel shock. "You look awful," she says, inspecting his face. "You poor dear, you've been in a war. Is *that* how they treat gentlemen in the countryside?" She takes off his hat and brushes his hair with her hand. "We've had a crisis here, too," she says. "Benchley messed the carpet, and the vet says it has to do with his age. We can't go on cleaning up the carpet because our dog is senile. I'd like a suggestion." She pauses. "Well, dear, did you find your lovely little barn?"

"I found it," he says. "I'll discuss everything after a shower and a martini." He begins to walk toward the stairs, then notices that he is tracking in mud and dirt on the front-hall carpet. He returns to the front entryway to wipe his shoes.

An hour later he is sitting in the den, sipping his second martini. He feels conspiratorial with the books and the furniture. "My God, it was hot," he says. "I don't know how those people stand it."

"You sound like Marco Polo," she says.

"I might as well be. They were looking at me. As if *I* were a sideshow. I didn't care much for it."

"You don't have to care for it. It's a hobby. You're supposed to *enjoy* a hobby, you know. Well, are you going to leave me in suspense forever? Where's the famous picture?" At this moment Benchley pads into the room and settles with a groan in his favorite corner. Jane glares at the dog, then sighs. "Let me see what you did," she says.

"I'll bring it in if you promise you've had enough gin to feel uncritical."

"I promise."

Walter goes to his car, lifts out the painting from the backseat, and brings it back into the den, setting it on the couch so that the light from the window illuminates it. He hears Vernice, the cook, tapping dishes in the kitchen.

Jane gazes at his painting for a long time. At last she says, "Well, it's not Velasquez, but it's very nice. School-of-Hopper, or somebody like that. You still have your touch. I had almost forgotten. But what's all this?" She points to the middle of the painted field.

"What?"

"This."

"What do you mean, 'this'?"

"This figure."

"There's no figure there. What figure?"

"Where I'm pointing to. It's almost like a ghost, green in the middle of green, standing there with its arms clasped. You've painted someone here. In the distance, small, but *I* can see him. I don't mean *much* of someone, just the outlines. Just a few lines."

Walter looks down where she is pointing but sees nothing but what he has drawn to indicate the field. "You're seeing things."

"No, I'm certainly *not* seeing things. *This* is a figure." She waits. "And quite an unpleasant figure, too, I would say. Look at how it's standing. It's not a woman or a man, it's an in-between, this thing. Why on earth did you paint this? Was there someone out there?"

"Of course not."

She turns toward him, and her face is set. "You think I'm making this up? I'm not. How can you be so blind to it? Should we call up the Erlandsons? They'll be home." She looks through the curtains at the side window toward the neighbors' yard. "Yes. They're home. Let me give them a buzz."

"No," he says, but she is already dialing.

"Irene? Jane. Listen, darling, would you and Ted do us a neighborly favor? No, no, we're just fine. It's just that Walter's brought back his first painting from the wilderness and . . . " She waits. "Yes, dear, a painting. He *paints*, for heaven's sake. No, I'm *not* joking. Anyway, we disagree about what's in it." She laughs politely. "Yes, in the *picture*, darling." Another pause. "No, it's not abstract, silly. It's a picture of a *barn*." She is interrupted but then continues. "Yes, on a farm. One of those. It looks like a barn, all right, but there's a field, and we've been having a tiny spat about the field. We need two brilliant and impartial art critics like you and Ted. No, I'm not joking. Please come over. There's a drink in it for you if you help us out."

Standing in front of Walter's painting, giving off a faint odor of Chivas Regal, Ted Erlandson offers a first tentative opinion. "I didn't know you were an artist, Walt. I must say, this is very impressive. Not beginner's work. And very, um, picturesque."

"I was an artist in college."

"Who wasn't? I was an actor. We all had talent, years ago. But you've been sitting on yours all this time. Imagine making all the money you've made when you could have been alone, starving in a garret, eating catsup and cottage cheese and living the life of bohemia." He turns to Irene. "Did you know we had such a talented neighbor?"

Irene shakes her head. "No. I certainly did not. Walter has always kept it a secret from me. And I thought he had no secrets." Irene Erlandson throws back her head and laughs; she is a tall woman, almost six feet, and her laugh sounds electrically amplified. "I thought he was just like us," she says, and sips her drink. "Mmmm, this is delicious, Walter. You could take up bartending if your new vocation fails you. Now, what're we supposed to be looking for?"

Walter says, "Jane sees something in the picture."

Jane transfers her drink to her left hand and points. "You see Walter's field, here? Well, do you see this figure? This sort of person with its horrible hands clasped in front of it, in the distance? This creature? You do see it, don't you?"

Irene scowls at the painting and shrugs. Ted closes one eye and looks puzzled. Then he nods. "Sure. Okay. If you say so."

"No," Jane says. "Look. You *must* see it."

"Well . . ." Irene nods. "It's there and it isn't. Like those vases that are faces and then are vases." She giggles. "You know, when I was a little girl, I used to wake up and see camel shapes in the folds of my bedroom curtains."

"Ted?" Jane gazes at him.

Ted Erlandson also shrugs and nods. "Okay, maybe I see it. I think you have a case, Jane. A definite case." He smiles. "I wouldn't've seen it if you hadn't told me it was there, but now that you mention it, I suppose it *is* there."

Looking at his own painting, Walter can almost see what she is talking about. And then he can't.

One week later he is sitting next to Minnehaha Creek, his easel in front of him. Once again the insects annoy him. Impatiently, Walter outlines the stones, the sand, the logs, the leaves, and the water.

Two days later, when he is mostly finished with it, he shows it to Jane, again during the cocktail hour. She examines it a long time.

"Oh my," she says finally with admiration. "I like this one much better than the other one. Technically, I mean. So many more difficulties here."

Walter nods.

"With all those different textures," she says, moving her pale hand with its diamond ring across the canvas as if in slow motion, "you had a much more difficult job." She stops and breathes in deeply. "Walter."

"What?"

"*Look* at this," she says emphatically, then points. "Look at what you've put into the water. Walter, dear, *why* are you doing this? Is it a joke? A joke on me?"

He looks where she is pointing. "What do you see this time?"

"It's not a matter of what *I* see, my darling. It's a matter of what is *there*. Of course you see it. Of course."

"No," he says, "I don't. Sorry." Benchley walks into the room, and Walter pats the dog on the head.

"This face," Jane says, looking at him. "This terrible face."

"Where?"

"Look! For pity's sake, look at what you've done!" Her voice is rising. "This face! Down under the water, between those stones! It looks like it's *screaming*. How can you say it isn't there when it's there for all to see? It's like Munch, under-water. And," she continues, "it's worse, because you've put this horrible thing in a babbling brook, in the center of this nice forest, with all this lovely dappled sun around. I don't believe you didn't know what you were doing this time."

Gazing at his painting, at the silent shouting watery face

Jane claims is there, he says, "You have to believe me when I tell you that I can't see it."

"Well." She pulls a handkerchief out of her sleeve. "I don't know if I believe you."

"Why shouldn't you?"

"It seems like a joke." She examines her fingernails. "You gave up a good career to paint these . . . these Rorschach blots in oils. Walter, dear, I wish you'd stop."

"But I've been enjoying it," he lies.

"I don't know," she says. "Maybe you have cataracts."

"Cataracts," he says. "I don't think so."

"Then where are these *things* coming from?" she asks. "You say *you* don't know. *I* don't know. But I can tell you how I feel. I feel as though these things are making fun of me."

"They're not."

"Then don't paint anymore!" She holds the handkerchief up and blows her nose. "Don't paint until you can paint a picture that doesn't have this dreadfulness in it. I'm sorry, dear, but that's how I feel. Can we talk about something else now? I want to go into the dining room and have our dinner as we usually do. We'll have a pleasant time. We won't say any more about this. Is that all right?" She looks at him. "Please?"

He looks at her face. Her expression is on the edge of desperation.

"I'll think about it," he says. When he glances away from her face, he sees that she glitters: her fingers and wrists, where the jewels are positioned to catch the light, have their lines of age, their own creases. The usual liver spots dot her hand. "Yes," he says at last. "Let's do that."

Now, a week later, he is driving his Buick Electra across the flatlands of central Minnesota, his white canvas, easel, and paints stored in the trunk, his two paintings in the backseat. A map is unfolded next to him, and he sees that the road he is on appears on the map as no more than a thin gray line, almost invisible. He cannot remember where that farm was or how he found his way there, to that wretched barn. He taps his right index finger on the map, following the rhythms of Bach on the radio. This music is growing fainter, and soon it will be gone. He turns the dial to a blank spot on the band, where he can listen to the random static, which calms him.

Listening to static, driving down a dirt road with no particular goal, lost, Walter sees the barn in the distance, his subject. By now it is midafternoon, cloudy, with no wind. He stops the car at the side of the road and opens the window. The smell of dirt and heavy moist air enters the car and mixes with the scent of leather and carpeting. For five minutes Walter gazes at the barn he once painted and at the farmhouse nearby. Where is Jane's ghost that found its way into his painting? He is feeling irritable and moody. Finally he opens the door, steps out into the road, and takes in both hands the two paintings he had placed on the backseat.

When he reaches the house, he presses the doorbell. There are patterns in the dust of the driveway. He looks at them. He sees a dog, and then a plant. Then a fabric of broken twigs.

"Yes?" It is the boy again, looking down at Walter through his glasses from behind the screen door.

"Hello," Walter says. "I don't think you'll remember me. I'm the man who—"

The boy interrupts him. "Sure. I remember. You painted our barn."

"That's right." Walter looks at the boy through the screen. The boy's face through the mesh has taken on a colorless rural-Seurat appearance of textured points. In the background Walter can hear a radio playing Bach, the same station that faded out in his car. Who listens to Bach in a farmhouse? He says, "I have the point . . . " He stops. "The *painting* with me. Right here."

"Are you tryin' to sell it? I don't think we can buy it." The boy puts his hands in his pockets. "I'm sure about that. We don't have much money right now."

From another part of the house, a woman shouts, "Who is it, Davey?"

"It's that guy who painted our barn."

"What does he want now?"

"I think he wants to sell his painting or something."

Walter joins in. "No, no, I don't! I don't want to sell it! I'm just here to show it to you!"

Now the woman appears behind the boy, her face, like his, patterned by the screen. "How do you do?" she says, wiping her hands on a towel. "I'm real sorry, but we're busy." He stares at her: her face, bland, blank, and pale, is totally illegible.

"May I come in?"

"What do you want?"

"I want to . . . I really must show you the painting."

"Please," she says. He isn't sure how to interpret this word. Therefore he opens the door, which squeaks like a parakeet, and steps inside.

"I appreciate this," he says. "You don't know my name. I am Walter Lundholm, and I'm retired, and I've taken up painting as my hobby. I live in the city. I used to be a real estate developer. I'm *not* asking for your money. What I wanted to do was, I wanted to show you the painting I did of your barn."

"Well," she says, "come into the living room."

He crosses the porch with its four rocking chairs and small pile of *National Geographic*s and steps into the hallway to the kitchen. On the wall is a picture of Jesus speaking to a group of American schoolchildren, and to the side is a finished wood table and four stainless-steel chairs with pink plastic cushions. The linoleum is midway between blue and gray. The living room is dominated by a console television set and a calendar from an auto-parts store, which has an illustration of a mountain lake whose water is a thick granular blue. Walter remains standing.

"Your husband?"

"Upstairs. He's sick."

"I know it," Walter says. "I think I want to give these pictures to him."

She places her right hand under her throat, the thumb on one side of the neck, the fingers on the other. "He's sick," she repeats. Walter looks at her again: when she stands, she seems to lean backward, to stand against things.

"I wonder if I might go upstairs with these paintings," he says.

At that moment, they hear a voice, from the second floor, which sounds as if it is coming over the radio. "Joyce," he shouts, but only with enough strength to make the shout achieve the level of slightly intensified speech, "who's there? Who're you talking to?"

"It's this man. Says he wants to give you two paintings he did."

There is a long pause, as if the voice is trying to gather some energy. Then he says, "Send him up."

Walter smiles for a split second. How much this procedure resembles the elaborate mannerisms of a business conference! Closed door, secretary, waiting period in the outer office: they have it all. The woman, Joyce, seems displeased by her husband's willingness to invite Walter upstairs. Sullenly, she guides him toward the stairway by holding her left arm out stiffly and walking toward the brown banister. In her rigid position is the suggestion that she might fall, but instead of falling she simply grasps the rail with her thin freckled fingers. Then she waits with her eyes down while Walter climbs the creaking stairs, one painting in either hand.

As he climbs, he feels time slowing down unpleasantly. He has never felt so silly in his life. At least, he thinks, I didn't buy a beret. Nevertheless, he wants to drop the paintings on the stairs and rush straightaway out of this house, past Joyce, past the boy in his orthopedic shoes. As he glances down to see if he would have a clear escape, he expects to see the woman scowling at him and blocking his path, but her place has been taken by the boy, who now has a birdhouse in his hands, held there as an offer of interest: look at what I have. Walter nods, as if to say that he'll look at it when he's finished.

At the top of the stairs, Walter feels a pang in his knees. He takes a deep breath. The second floor is rich in the fetid odor of medicine and bedclothes, and something meant to disguise it, the sugary wintergreen stink of air freshener.

"In here," the voice says from the one darkened room facing the front of the house. Walter looks into the first room, the boy's, and sees photographs of birds scissored out of popular magazines and scotch-taped to the walls: sparrows, juncos, wrens, crested flycatchers, owls, pheasants, egrets, and on one wall scores of bluebirds, a collage of photos from floor to ceiling, apparently cut out of bird books. On this wall in the middle of the bluebirds is a left-profile picture of Jesus. "I said I'm in here," the voice rasps irritably. Walter advances into the room.

The man of the house lies propped in bed, lips drawn back over his teeth, his skin the color of school paste. He does not turn his head, though he holds out his thin knuckled hand for Walter to shake. Shaking this thin hand makes the hair on the back of Walter's neck stand up. The man in bed is wasting away. He is a male Medusa: sunken eyes and hair like watercress. Medicines are scattered on a bedside table, and a television set on the other side of the room is tuned to a rerun of *The Honeymooners*, the sound so low that only Ralph is audible, as he points his finger straight in the air and shouts at Alice.

"Hello," Walter says. "I'm sorry to intrude on you."

The man nods. "I know you."

"Yes. Yes, you do. I want to give you the picture I painted," Walter says.

"You do."

"Yes."

"Well, it's not much good to me," the man says. "My health ain't too hot right now." He waits, tugging at the sheets. "Still and all, if you want to give me your picture, I guess it's none of my business." The smell in the room makes Walter want to gag. The man in bed points down. "That it?"

Walter holds up the painting so that it is displayed on the foot of the bed. The farmer stares at it a long time.

"You did that."

"Yes."

Walter waits for a pardon. Just then the man says, "It's nice." Before he can respond to this compliment, the man continues in a half-whisper. "It's nice for someone to do up your place like that. You know, I worked here since I was twenty." Walter tries to nod. He feels the presence of the man's wife watching from the doorway. The farmer continues talking. "I like it. You painted this place like it was important. A fellow from the city. Well, fine. I want you to know I appreciate it." The effort to say all this makes him sink down into bed.

"Thank you," Walter says. "I have another one here of a stream." He holds it up.

The farmer stares at it. "That's nice, too."

"If you want it," Walter says, "it's yours. My wife doesn't like it. She doesn't like the other one either. She doesn't want them in the house. My wife," Walter says, "doesn't like nature."

"Too bad."

"Well, you can have them both. Free."

The man does not smile, but he nods again. "Thank you. Joyce'll put the picture of the barn up on the wall. I never had a painting before. We were too busy."

Walter nods.

"But anyway," the farmer says, beginning to wave Walter away, "I appreciate your coming out here and I only wish I

132   CHARLES BAXTER

could get up and offer you a beverage." He is staring at the painting of his barn. "But I can't. I'm real sick, y'know." Walter nods again, idiotically. "That's a nice thing, that barn," he says, "and thank you." He holds out his hand again, and Walter stares at it, dreading to grasp it, but at last he does, and on cue the hairs on the back of his neck stand up. "Goodbye."

"Goodbye." He steps past Joyce, who doesn't move out of his way, and is heading down the stairs, his eyes half closed, when he sees the boy, who still holds the birdhouse in his hands.

"You talk to my dad?" the boy asks, but before Walter can answer, the boy says, "This is something I made downstairs in the basement during my free time. It's too small for squirrels, and chipmunks don't want it. I'm going to put it up on the catalpa outside the kitchen window even though the wrens aren't going to come and use it until springtime." He hands the birdhouse to Walter, who examines it and hands it back. But this gesture is not enough. The boy holds it up to Walter's eye level. "See?" he asks. The wren house is painted blue, the same shade as the kitchen linoleum.

"Yes," Walter says.

"Davey," Joyce calls at the top of the stairs, "don't bother the man. Take him out to his car, would you?"

"Okay, Mom." The boy tucks the birdhouse under his left arm and marches through the living room out onto the porch, and out through the porch into the front yard. "We don't get too many birds around here," the boy says as he walks. "Last week I saw a scarlet tanager. It was on its way somewhere. Only the sparrows and chickadees stay around here. And the bluejays and the crows. They're related, did you know that?" He stops and turns around. "Did you give my dad a picture of the barn?"

"Yes," Walter says.

"I bet he really likes it."

Now Walter is standing by his car while the boy continues his monologue about birds. The house sparrow, he says, was introduced into North America by travelers from Europe. In some places, the boy continues, the sparrow was once considered a messenger of news from the gods. If you put a sparrow into a cage, it will not chirp. A princess was once turned into a sparrow by her father, in a story. The state bird of Minnesota is the loon. When it flies, its big feet are stretched out past the tail. They're hard to spot on lakes. When they dive, they can stay under for a minute. Finches are easier to see, what with their yellow and purple color, and their nesting rituals. And their song is easy to remember. Suddenly the boy puckers his mouth and sings: *swit-wit-wit*.

"I don't know anything about birds," Walter says. "At the end of the day, I don't look for a bird. I look for a martini. Did you know," he says, staring at the boy, "that many people now put ice cubes into their martinis? That's a great mistake. Martinis are meant to be poured straight up, preferably with an olive in the glass, and sipped. Poured," he says, wiping his forehead with his sleeve, staring toward the dusty dirt road, on which a red pickup truck is now passing, "from a silver cocktail shaker, with condensation from the air beaded on the sides. *That's* what I want right now, young man. A drink."

"We don't drink here."

"I believe it." He walks toward his car. "Actually, I do know something about birds. They are the most beautiful of God's creations." The boy begins to nod, then stops himself. Walter makes his way to his car, and suddenly the boy begins talking about woodpeckers. Walter opens the car door and slides in behind the wheel while the boy is still in midsentence. He manages to wave and starts the car. As he drives off, he looks in the rearview mirror to see the boy observing his departure. The boy doesn't look like a bird; he doesn't even suggest the image of a bird.

Driving back to Minneapolis, Walter considers his retirement plans. He has no more mental images of paintings he wants to paint. He has no idea of what he will do with his time. Start a business, he thinks, turning on the radio. A new business. Building wren houses, using low-cost lumber.

He is almost inside the city limits when he sees traffic slowing down in his lane. For fifteen minutes he crawls and creeps forward, until he reaches the source of the trouble, an accident. The ambulance has arrived; one car is accordioned in front; another is turned over. Broken glass everywhere on the pavement, a cop gesturing him past. Men bent over. Over what? Walter keeps his eyes fixed ahead and inches forward until the congestion clears. He accelerates, rushing home.

The Eleventh Floor

>‹‹

Carefully drunk, Mr. Bradbury sat on his patio-balcony in the bland morning sunshine, sipping vodka-and-something. He was waiting for his son to visit. This son, Eric, had called and said he would arrive shortly, and that was an hour ago. It was Saturday: vodka day. He peered down from the eleventh floor at the sidewalk trees, where the sparrows were making a racket. Below the sparrows, Mr. Bradbury could see the velvet brown dot of the doorman's hat. He thought he could smell crab-apple blossoms and something more subtle, like dust.

In shivering glassy clarity, he observed a rusting blue Vega park in front of a fireplug. That would be Eric, who had a collection of parking tickets, little marks of risk and daring. Watching him lock his Vega, his father mashed out his cigarette in a blue pottery ashtray balanced on the balcony railing. He coughed, putting his hand in front of his mouth. Eric had stopped to talk to the doorman, George. George and Eric, two human dots. Eric's pinpoint face turned, tilted, and stared up at the rows of balconies, finding his father on the eleventh. He did not wave.

Standing up, Mr. Bradbury tested his reflexes. He bent his knees and thought of a line from Byron: "From the dull palace to the dirty hovel, something something something novel." The problem with poetry was that you were always having to look it up. He couldn't recall which poem contained the dull palace, nor did he care. He stepped out of the sunlight into the living room and sank into the sofa, trying not to groan. Elena, the Peruvian housekeeper, was preparing lunch, probably one of her crude ethnic casseroles. She didn't inform him of her plans in advance. He reached over to the coffee table and pressed the mute button on the remote control to silence the Cable News Network announcer. His neck hurt. He rubbed it, and to his own fingers the skin felt scaly. At least no swellings or lumps. He let his right arm drop down onto the side table. His thumb landed in the engraved silver scallop-shell ashtray and emerged from it with a gray coating of ash. He bent over and was rubbing the thumb on the carpet just as his son knocked.

The boy had a key; the knock was some kind of ritual announcement of estrangement. He heaved himself up to his feet and, remembering to stand straight, made his way past the bookshelves and the paintings to the foyer.

"Eric," he said, opening the door and seeing his son in a blast of sentimental pride. "I'm glad you came." The flaring of his love made him shy, so that he drew back his body even as he extended his hand. Eric shook his hand, gazed down at his father's face with an examining look, and sniffed twice. Mr. Bradbury could tell that Eric was trying to catch the scent of his breath. "Come in, come in," he said. "Don't loiter out there in the hall. Why didn't you just let yourself in with your key?"

"I lost it," Eric said. "I lost all my keys."

"Where?"

"I don't know. A party. Yeah, that's right. A party."

Eric stood in the center of the living room, checking out the familial furniture. Then he tossed his jacket on a chair and bent down to unlace his shoes. For some reason his father noticed that his son was wearing thick white cotton socks. Then Eric straightened up, pleased to be on display, his thumbs hooked in the back pockets of his jeans.

"You're getting sizable. Is it the swimming?"

"Not this season," Eric said. "It's track. They had us on a training program."

"I always forget what a big kid you are. I don't remember anyone in the family being your size except your mother's Uncle Gus, who worked in the Water Department. He had the worst halitosis I've ever encountered in an adult human being. Your mother used to say that he smelled like a Labrador with stomach lesions." He smiled as his son walked toward the open porch door and the balcony. It was an athletic, pantherish walk. "You let your hair grow," his father said. "You have a beard. You look like a Renaissance aide-de-camp."

Eric reached over for the ashtray on the railing and fastidiously put it down on the deck. Without turning around, he said, "I thought I'd try it out." Mr. Bradbury saw him glance at his drink, measuring it, counting the ice cubes.

"Try what? Oh. The beard. You should. Absolutely."

Eric lifted himself easily and sat on the railing, facing his father. He hooked his feet around the bars. He squinted toward the living room, where his father stood. "Did it surprise you?"

"What?" The beard: he meant the beard. "Oh, a bit, maybe. But I'm in a state of virtually constant surprise. George surprises me with tales of his riotous family, you surprise me with your sudden visits, and Elena out there in the kitchen surprises me every time she manages to serve me a meal. Your old dad lives in a state of paralyzed amazement. So. How's college life? You've been kind of short on the letters."

"It's only across town, Dad."

"I know how far away it is. You could call. You could put your finger on the old rugged dial."

"I forget. And so do you." Eric put his arms out and leaned his head back to catch the rays of the sun. If he fell, he'd fall eleven floors.

"In that sunlight," his father said, "your skin looks shellacked."

Eric eyed his father, then the patio deck, where the glass of vodka and fruit juice made a small festive group with the ashtray, a Zippo lighter, and an FM transistor radio. "Shellacked?"

Mr. Bradbury put his hands in his pockets. He took three

steps forward. "I only meant that you look like you've already had some sun this year. That's all I meant." He laughed, one rushed chuckle. "I will not have my vocabulary questioned." He stepped onto the balcony and sat down in a canvas chair, next to the drink and the cigarettes. "Do you ever write your sister?"

"I call her. She's okay. She asks about you. Your health and things like that." Mr. Bradbury was shading his eyes. "How's your breathing?"

"My breathing?" Mr. Bradbury took his hand away from his eyes. "Fine. Why do you ask?"

"It seems sort of shallow or something."

"You were never much for tact, were you, kid?" His father leaned back. "I don't have emphysema yet, if that's the question. But I still smoke. Oh, yes." He smiled oddly. "Cigarettes," he said, "are my friends. They have the faith."

Eric hopped down, so that he was no longer looking at his father, and turned to survey the city park two blocks west. "How's business?"

His father waved his hand in a gesture that wasn't meant to express anything. "Good. Business is good. I'm doing commercials for a bank owned by a cartel of international slime, and I also have a breakfast-food account now, aimed at kids. Crispy Snax. The demographics are a challenge. We're using animated cartoons and we've invented this character, Colonel Crisp, who orders the kids to eat the cereal. He raises a sword and the product appears in a sort of animated blizzard of sugar. We're going for the Napoleonic touch. It's coercive, of course, but it's funny if you're positioned behind the joke instead of in front of it. We're getting angry letters from mothers. We must be doing something right." He stared at his son's back. "Of course, I get tired sometimes."

"Tired?"

He waited, then said, "I don't know. I should take a vacation." He looked past his son at the other buildings across the street with their floors of patio-balconies, some with hanging plants, others with bicycles. "So I could recollect sensations sweet in hours of weariness 'mid the din of towns and cities. Listen, you want a drink? You know where it is."

Eric turned and stared at his father. "Eleven-thirty in the morning?" He lifted himself on the railing again.

Mr. Bradbury shrugged. "It's all right. It's Saturday. It warms up the mental permafrost. On weekends it's okay to drink before lunch. I've got a book here that says so."

"You *wrote* that book, Pop."

"Well, maybe I did." He sat up. "Damn it, stop worrying about me. *I* don't worry about *you*. You're too young to be worrying about me, and besides, I'm making out like a bandit."

Eric said nothing. He was looking away from his father into the living room, at a Lichtenstein print above the sofa. It showed a comic-book woman passionately kissing a comic-book man.

"You won't mind if I do?"

"What?" Eric said. "Have a drink? No, I won't mind."

Mr. Bradbury stood up and walked to the kitchen, remembering to aim himself and to keep his shoulders thrown back. "Your semester must be about done," he said, his voice raised above the sound of ice cubes clattering out of the tray. "How much longer?"

"Two weeks."

"You taking that lifeguarding job again this summer?"

"That's part of what I came to talk to you about."

"Oh." In a moment he returned with what was identifiably a screwdriver. "Cheers," he said, raising it. "I knew there must be some reason." He settled down into the chair, reached over for the ashtray and lighter, and lit a cigarette. "How's your love life? How's the bad Penny?"

"Penny and I split."

"You and Penny split up? I wasn't informed." He took a sip of the drink, inhaled from the cigarette, then laughed. Smoke came out his mouth as he did. "I'm going to miss that girl, wandering around here in her flower-pattern pajamas, her little feet sinking into the carpet, and asking me in broken French my opinions of Proust. *'Monsieur Bradbury, aimez-vous Proust?' 'Oh, oui, Penny. Proust, c'est un écrivain très diligent.'*" He waited, but his son didn't smile. "Was she an inattentive lover?"

"Jesus Christ, Dad." Eric picked at something beneath the hair on his right forearm. "You can't ask about that."

"Sure I can. You asked about my breathing. So what was the problem? Wasn't she assiduous enough for you?"

"Assiduous?" Eric thought for a moment. "Yeah yeah. She was assiduous enough. She was good in bed. Is that what you want to know? She was fine. That's not why we split."

Eric's father was brushing the top of his head with the palm of his hand. "You know, Eric, I envy you. I suffer from *Glückschmerz*: the envy we feel upon hearing of the good fortune of others."

Eric nodded. "I know it, Pop." He jumped down from the railing a second time and sat next to his father, so that they would both be looking at the building across the street and the rest of the city's skyline, not at each other. "I have this other girl now. I think I love her."

Mr. Bradbury watched an airplane off in the distance and began to hum "In a Sentimental Mood."

"Did you hear me? I said I was in love."

"I heard you." He took another sip of his drink and then reached for the cigarette. "Sure, I heard you. I've been hearing about all the women you've fallen in love with since you were sixteen. No, fifteen. Almost six years now. That's the price I pay for an amorous son. What's her name this time?"

"Lorraine."

"Lorraine." He smiled. "Ah, sweet Lorraine. The Cross of Lorraine. Alsace-Lorraine. You two aren't married, are you?"

"No, we aren't married. Why?"

"To what," his father asked, "do I owe the honor of this visit?"

"Oh, come on, Pop." Mr. Bradbury felt his son's hand on his knee. The gesture made him feel ninety-two years old. "It's not that. I'm going to be asking you for money."

"Oh, and when will that be?"

"In about thirty minutes." His son waited. "It'd be impolite to ask before that."

"You do know how to close a deal. Wait until the old man is in his cups. So it's not bad news after all."

"No, Dad, it's not bad news. It's—"

He stopped when Elena called them to the table. It was not an ethnic casserole. She'd prepared ham with salad and asparagus in hollandaise sauce. Eric's father carried his drink and his cigarettes over to the table and placed them carefully next to his engraved silver napkin ring. "Putting on the ritz for you here today," he said. "Isn't Elena a swell woman?" he asked loudly, so that she'd hear. "You'll love this meal!" he almost shouted.

"Cut out the shit, Pop," Eric said, whispering. "I can't stand it."

"Okeydoke." He sat back and with one eye shut examined the wine bottle Elena had put on the table. "Chateau Smith, '69. An obscure California wine, heh heh. I think you'll like it." He swallowed part of his drink, put the glass aside, then picked up his fork and pushed a slice of ham around on the plate. "So. What's the money for? I thought you *had* some money. I hope to God you aren't one of these young goddamn entrepreneurs. I'd hate that." He took a bite. "I wouldn't join the bourgeois circus a minute before I had to."

"I'm not. This is for getting away."

"Getting away from what?" He chewed. "There's no getting away from anything."

"Yes, there is. I want to live up north in the woods near Ely for a year."

"You want to do *what*?" Eric's father put down his fork and stared at his son, an astonished smile breaking across his face. "I don't believe it. Is *that* what you came here to tell me? You want to go off into the woods and live like a rustic?" He threw back his head and laughed. "Oh my God," he said. "Rousseau lives." He sat chuckling, then turned to Eric again. "Let me guess. You want to discover yourself. You want to discover *who you are*. You and this Lorraine have been having deep sinister whispered talks far into the night, and she thinks you need to find your authentic blah blah blah blah blah. Am I right so far?"

Eric scowled at his father, holding himself silent. His big hands fidgeted with the silverware. Then he said, "Lorraine just suggested it. What I want is to get away from college and the city . . . and this." He swept his hand to indicate his father's dinner table, apartment, and the view outside the eleventh floor. "Lorraine's family has a cabin up north, and I want to live there this winter and work close by, if I can find a job. That's what I want for a year." He was staring intently at his fork.

"I see. You don't want to end up middle-aged and red-eyed."

Eric pretended not to hear. "Lorraine's staying down here in the city. Her family's letting me use their place. It's for myself."

Eric's father took his lower lip in his teeth as he smiled. Then he said, "I didn't think your generation indulged in such hefty idealism. I thought they were all designing computers and snorting the profits gram by gram. But this, a rustication, living in cabins and searching the soul, why, it's positively

Russian. With that beard, you even look slightly Russian. Who've you been reading, Thoreausky?"

"I've read Thoreau," Eric said, looking out the window.

"I bet you have," his father said. "Look, kid, I'm very pleased. No kidding. Just make one promise. While you're up there, read some Chekhov. If you're going to be a Russian, that's the kind of Russian to be. Skip the other claptrap. You promise?"

"Sure. If you want me to."

"Yup," his father said. "I do." He paused. His arms and shoulders ached. Every time he ate, he felt a hard lump in his stomach. He furtively touched his neck, then glanced at Eric, shoveling in the food, and said, "If your mother were still alive, I'd be getting all riled up and telling you to get settled down and finish your studies and all that sort of thing. Mothers don't like it when their sons go off sulking into the woods. She'd've been worried. But you can handle yourself. And frankly I think it's a great idea." He leaned back. "'Season of mists and mellow fruitfulness,'" he said. "Keats. I once used it in an ad for the Wisconsin State Board of Tourism. It's the wrong season, but the thought's right. Go north before you get tired."

"Tired?"

Mr. Bradbury wiped his mouth with his napkin and stared vaguely at the television set next to the sideboard. It, too, was tuned to CNN. He could no longer resist alcoholic gloom. "You'll get tired someday," he said. "Like a damaged mainspring. You'll get home at night and stand in front of the window as the sun sets. You'll always know what time it is without looking at your watch. You'll see odd mists you can't identify coming up from the pond in the park. There's a pattern in those mists, but you won't find it. Then the fraud police knock on your door. Those bastards won't leave a man alone."

"Pop, you drink too much."

Mr. Bradbury's face reddened. "If we weren't pals," he

said, "I'd sock you in the nose. Listen, kid. When I'm sober I don't mortify people with the known facts of life. But you're family." He rose from the table and walked unsteadily across the thick carpeting of the living room. In five minutes he returned, carrying a check and waving it in the air as if to dry the ink. "A huge sum," he said. "The damaged fruits of a sedentary life. If you don't find work right away, you can read and bum around in the woods with the other unemployed animals on the dole. If you *do* find a job, which I doubt, since it's a depressed area, you can refund the unused portion. Someday you can pay this back. That's the convention between fathers and sons."

"I'll try to come down at Christmas."

"Wouldn't that be nice." Mr. Bradbury cut a spear of his asparagus into small pieces and picked up the tip with his fork. The check was in the middle of the table, and Eric reached out and picked it up, folding it into his trouser pocket.

"Good," his father said. "You didn't lunge." He didn't look up. "You have a picture of this Lorraine?"

"No. Sorry. Are you seeing anybody yourself?"

His father shrugged. "There's a woman in Chicago I visit every month or so. Or she comes here. Someone I met through business. A small affair. Morgan, her name is. Her children are grown up, same age as you. She has a pretty laugh. The thought of that laugh has gotten me through many a desperate week. We're thinking of embarking on a short cruise together in the Caribbean this winter." He stopped. "But it's all quite pointless." He rubbed his forehead. "On the other hand, maybe it isn't. I'll be damned if I know what it is."

After lunch they made small talk, then went into the living room. Just before Eric left, his father said, "You snob, you never call. You always wait for me to do it. It's beggarly and humiliating. You never invite me over to your sordid lair. It irritates me." He was staring at the television screen, where a man was applying shaving cream to a bathroom mirror. "I don't like to be the one who calls all the damn time." He sneezed. "Still collecting parking tickets?"

"Still doing it. Dad, I gotta go. Lorraine's expecting me later this afternoon. I'll be in touch."

"Right." He started to extend his hand, thought better of it, and stood up. He held out his arms and embraced his son. He was four inches shorter than Eric, and when they drew together, his son's thick beard brushed against his face. "Be sure to call," he said. Eric nodded, turned around, and hurried toward the door. "Don't you dare hold me in contempt," he said inaudibly, under his breath.

With his hand on the doorknob, Eric shouted backward, "Thanks for the money, Dad. Thanks for everything."

Then he was gone.

Mr. Bradbury stood in the same position until he heard the elevator doors close. Then he backed into the living room and stood for a moment watching the television screen. He turned off the set. In his study, he bent down at the desk and subtracted two thousand dollars from the balance in his checking account. He glanced at the bookshelves above his desk, reached for a copy of Chekhov's stories and another volume, Keats's poems, put them on the desk, then walked down the hallway to the front closet. He put on a sweater and told Elena he was stepping out for a few minutes.

He crossed the street and headed for the park. In the center of this park was a pond, and on the far side of the water was a rowboat concession. He counted the rowboats in the pond: twelve. Feeling the onset of hangover, he strolled past some benches, reaching into his shirt pocket for a breadstick he had stashed there for the ducks. As he walked, he broke up the bread and threw it into the water, but the water was littered with bread and the ducks didn't notice him.

When he reached the rowboat concession, he paid a twenty-five-dollar deposit and left his driver's license as security, then let the skinny acned attendant fit him for an orange life jacket. He carried the two oars in either hand and eased himself into the blue rowboat he'd been assigned. He tried breathing the air for the scent but could smell nothing but his own soured breath. Taking the oars off the dock, panting, he fit them into the oarlocks. Then, with his back to the prow of the boat, he rowed, the joints squeaking, out to the middle of the lake.

Once there, he lifted the oars and brought them over the gunwales. He listened. The city traffic was reduced to vague honks and hums; the loudest sounds came from the other boaters and from their radios. Taking a cigarette out of his sweater pocket, he gazed at his building, counting the floors until he could see his bedroom window. There I am, he thought. A rowboat went by to his right, with a young man sitting in front, and his girlfriend pulling at the oars. He watched them until they were several boat lengths away, and then he cursed them quietly. He flicked his cigarette into the water.

As he gazed at the west side of the pond, he noticed that the apple blossoms floating on the water had collected into a kind of clump. The water lapped against the boat. He bent over and with his right index finger began absentmindedly to write his name on the pond's pale-green surface. When he realized what he was doing, he started to laugh.

Eric called in September, November, and twice in December. In a remote and indistinct voice he said he wasn't having an easy time of it, living by himself. Two weeks before Christmas he announced that he had moved out of the cabin and was living in a rented room in Ely, where he worked as a stock boy in the IGA supermarket. He thought he would give the experiment another month and then call it quits. He said— as if it were incidental—that he had met another woman.

"What about Lorraine?" his father asked.

"That's over."

"It's a good thing you fall out of love as fast as you fall in. Who's the new one?"

"You'll meet her."

"I hope so."

In February, after a heavy snowstorm, Eric called again to say that he'd be down the following Saturday and would bring Darlene with him. "Darlene?" his father asked. "I knew a Darlene once. She ran a bowling alley."

"You should talk," his son said. "Wilford."

"All right, all right. I see your point. So you'll be here on Saturday. Looking forward to it. How long'll you stay?"

"How should I know?" his son said.

George buzzed the apartment to let him know that his son and his son's new girlfriend had just come in. Mr. Bradbury was waiting at the door when he heard the elevator slide open, and he went on waiting there, under the foyer's chandelier, while in the hallway Eric and Darlene worked out a plan. The only remark he could catch was his son's "Don't let him tell you . . . " He couldn't hear the rest of it. What to do, or what to think, or something of the sort.

After they knocked, he waited thirty seconds, timing it by his Rolex. When his son knocked a second time, harder and faster, he said, "I'm coming, I'm coming."

He opened the door and saw them: a surprised young couple. His son had shaved his beard and cut his hair short; the effect was to make him seem exposed and smalltownish. He looked past his father into the apartment with the roving gaze of a narcotics agent. "Hi, Dad," he said. The woman next to him looked at Eric, then at his father, waiting for them to shake hands or embrace; when they did neither, she said, "Hi, Mr. Bradbury," and thrust out her hand. "Darlene Spinney."

The hand was rough and chapped. She glanced into the apartment. "Pleased to meet you."

"Likewise," Eric's father said, moving aside so that they could step into the foyer. "Come in and warm up." Eric slipped off his parka, draped it over a chair, groaned, and immediately walked down the hallway to the bathroom. Mr. Bradbury helped Darlene with her coat, noting from the label that she had purchased it at Sears. The woman's figure was substantial, north-woods robust: capable of lifting canoes. "I wonder where that son of mine went to?"

"Eric?" She glanced down the hall. "He's in the bathroom. I'll tell you something, Mr. Bradbury: you make your son real nervous. He's as jumpy as a cat. What I think it is, he's got diarrhea, bringing me here and seeing you. That's two strikes. One more strike and the boy'll be out cold."

He looked at her with some interest. "Come into the living room, Miss Spinney," he said. "Care for a drink?"

"I don't know. Maybe a beer?"

"Sure." He leaned toward her. "I suppose my son has warned you about my drinking."

"What he said was you sometimes have hard stuff before lunch."

"That is correct." He went to the refrigerator, took out a Heineken's, and poured it into a glass. "That is what I do. But only on weekends. You can think of it as my hobby. Did he tell you anything else?"

"Oh, I asked, all right. Nothing much but mumbles."

"What'd you ask?"

"Well, for instance, did you get mean."

"When I drank."

"Right."

"Why'd you want to know?" He came out of the kitchen and handed the glass to her. They both walked toward the front window.

"Do you know mean drinkers, Mr. Bradbury? I don't guess

so. *I* know a few. In my family, this is. It's not nice conversation and I won't go through all the details, about being hit and everything. This," she said, looking out the window, "is different. I sort of figured you were a man who doesn't have to hit things."

"I never learned," he said, giving the words a resentful torque. "I hired people. Now where did you and Eric meet? I can't imagine."

"At the IGA. He was working in produce, and I was up there at the checkout. I'd never seen him in town before he started working in the back. Well, I mean." She looked for a place to set down her beer, hesitated, and held on to it. "I thought, oh, what a nice face. Two glances and you don't have to think about it. So we ate our lunches together. Traded cookies and carrots. He's nice. He gave me a parking ticket. He said it was an old joke? Anyway, we talked. He wasn't like the local boys."

"No?"

"No. He can sit by himself. When he works, he listens to the boss, Mr. Glusac, giving him orders, and he has this so-what look on his face. He's sweet. Like he's always making plans. He's a dreamer. Can't fix a car."

"I don't think he ever learned."

"That's the truth. Doesn't know what gaskets are, says he never learned to use a socket wrench. That Vega of his was hard-starting and dieseling, and I told him to tune it, you know, with a timing light, and he tells me he's never removed a sparkplug in his life. 'We didn't do that,' he says. Jesus, it's a long way down." She was gazing at the frozen pond in the park.

"Eleven floors," Mr. Bradbury said. "You can't hear the harlot's cry from street to street up here, more's the pity. I look down on it all from a great height. I have an eleventh-floor view of things."

She said, "I can see a man walking a dog. Eric says you write commercials." She sat down on the sofa and glanced at the muted newscaster on the television set. He noticed that her fingernails were painted bright red, and that the back of one hand was scarred. "Is it hard, writing commercials?"

"Not if your whole life prepares you to do it. And of course there are the anodynes. If it weren't for them, my heart wouldn't be in it."

"Anodynes."

"I'm sorry. Painkillers. Things that come in bottles and tubes."

"I only had a year of community college before I had to go to work," Darlene said, and just as Mr. Bradbury understood what her remark was supposed to explain, she said, "I'm always afraid I'm boring people. Eric says I don't bore him. Do you know your TV set is on?"

"Yes."

"Why's it on if you aren't listening to it?"

"I like to have someone in the room with me, in case I get a call from the fraud police. Ah, hey, here's the kid."

Eric had reappeared silently. His father turned to look at him; he might have been standing in the hallway, out of sight, listening to them both for the last five minutes. Eric sat down next to Darlene on the sofa, putting his arm around her shoulders. She snuggled close to him, and Mr. Bradbury resisted the impulse to close his eyes. He sat down in his Barcelona chair. "So," he began, with effort, "here you are. Give me a report. How was nature?"

"Nature was fine." With his free hand Eric brutally rubbed his nose. The nose was running, and he wiped his hand on the sofa.

"Fine? Did the flora and fauna suit you? I want a report. Did you discover yourself? Let's hear something about the pastoral panorama." Darlene, he noticed, was staring at his mouth.

"It was fine," Eric said, staring, without subtlety, at the ceiling.

"I hate it when you look at the ceiling. A world without

objects is a sensible emptiness. Come on, Eric, let's have a few details. Did you from outward forms win the passion and the life, whose fountains are within?"

"My dad is a quoter," Eric said. He glanced at Darlene. "He quotes." He saw his father looking at him. "It was fine," he repeated, facing his father.

"He won't talk about that time alone in that cabin, Mr. Bradbury, so you might as well not ask. Lord knows I've tried."

"Just between him and his psyche, eh?"

"'Psyche,'" Eric said, shaking his head. "Jesus Christ."

"There you go, criticizing my vocabulary again. When *will* I be allowed to use the six-dollar words they taught us at Amherst? Never, it appears." He smiled at Darlene. "Pay no attention to me. I inflict my irony on everybody."

A long pause followed. Eric's father had begun counting the seconds in groups of two when Darlene said, "You wouldn't believe all the city people who come up north to commune with nature. Like that woman Lorraine, *her* family. We see them all summer. They buy designer backpacks and dehydrated foods they don't eat. Then they sleep on the ground for two weeks, complain of colds, and whiz home in their station wagons. Me, I'm lucky if I can sleep in a bed."

"Darlene has insomnia," Eric explained.

"Right. I do. That's why I don't understand people sleeping on the ground. Who wants that when you can shower in a bathroom and sleep in a bed and look out from the eleventh floor? Not me."

"Insomnia," Mr. Bradbury said. "How interesting. Ever tried Dalmane or Ativan? Doriden isn't too bad either."

"You have insomnia?" she asked. "Try bananas. Or turkey. They have an enzyme, tryptophan, and that's what you need. Unless you're hard-core, like me. I have to run, eat bananas, skip coffee, but it usually doesn't make any difference."

"We jog together," Eric said.

They were cuddling there, Darlene and Eric, Mr. Bradbury decided, to test his powers of detachment. Before this was over he would be a Zen saint. He thought longingly of the vodka bottle in the kitchen cupboard, whose cap he had not, *not*, removed once today: his hands were folded in his lap, as he watched Darlene place her hand on Eric's leg. The truth, he thought, raising one hand to scratch his ear, is an insufferable test of a man's resources. Tilting his head imperceptibly, he glanced for relief at the Lichtenstein above the sofa. "Bananas?" he said.

"Eric says you wrote those Colonel Crisp commercials." Her voice was egging him on into the kitchen: glass, ice cubes, and the tender care of the liquor.

"Yes." He would not stand it. He *could* not stand it, and began to get up.

Darlene twisted around, so that Eric's hand fell off her shoulders onto the sofa, to look at the wall behind her. "What's that?" she asked.

"That? Oh, that's a Lichtenstein." He sat down again.

"Is it valuable?"

"Yes. I suppose so. Yes."

She was looking at it closely, probably, Mr. Bradbury thought, counting the dots in the woman's face. "Do you write radio commercials too?"

"Oh yes. I once wrote a spot for Westinghouse light bulbs with a Janáček fanfare in the background. *That* made them sit up."

"Jesus!" Eric stood suddenly. "I can't *stand* this!" He went down the hallway, and they both heard a door slam. Just then Elena came into the living room to announce that lunch was ready.

"It's a hard life up here on the eleventh floor," Mr. Bradbury mused. "Maybe he went to get a banana." He waited. "Or some white meat."

"I'll get him," Darlene said, rising. "His moods've never

bothered me. Did you know," she began, then stopped. She apparently decided to plunge ahead, because she said, "He talks a lot about his mother."

"Not to me. She died of cancer, you know."

"Yeah. He said so. He remembers all of it. He *likes* you, Mr. Bradbury. Don't get him wrong. He's crazy about you. I shouldn't say this."

"Oh, please say it. Crazy about me?"

"Oh sure. Didn't you know?" She looked surprised.

Mortified and pleased, he watched her disappear down the hall.

After lunch, whose terrain was crossed by Mr. Bradbury's painfully constructed comic anecdotes about daily work in an advertising agency, he suggested that they all go out for a walk in the park. Eric and Darlene agreed with an odd fervor. After bundling themselves up, they took the elevator down, Darlene checking her face, making moues, in the elevator's polished mirror.

Outside the temperature was ten degrees above zero, with no wind, and a sunny sky. When they reached the park, Darlene ran out ahead of them onto the pond, where the park authorities had cleared a rink for skating. A loudspeaker was playing Waldteufel.

"Don't lecture me," Eric said. "Don't tell me what I should or shouldn't be doing."

"Who, me?" Darlene was now out of earshot. "That's for suckers. Can you tell me yet how long you're staying?"

"Why do you keep asking? A few days. Then we're going north again. I'm going to be up there for the rest of the winter and then re-enroll next fall and graduate in the spring."

"I don't suppose she's going with you."

"I don't know." He waited. "She's interested in our money. *The* money."

"A good woman's failing. I kind of like her," Mr. Bradbury

said. "Diamond in the rough and all that. At first I thought she was queen of the roller derby. Didn't know if she was playing with a full deck."

"I almost proposed to her," Eric said. "Almost."

"Oh Christ." His father stomped his right foot in the snow. "You, with all your, well, call it potential, and you want to marry a girl who counts out change?"

She was far ahead of them on the ice, pulling two children on skates around in a circle. The children yelled with pleasure.

"She's . . . different, Pop. With her, everything's simpler. They don't have women like her around here, I don't think. You don't get what I mean at all."

"Oh, I get it. You went up north looking for nature, and you found it, and you brought it back, and there it, I mean she, is. Overbite, straight hair, chapped hands, whopping tits, and all."

"You wouldn't believe," Eric said, watching her, "how comforting she is."

"What?" He stopped and waited. "Well, I might."

"When I wake up, she's always awake. She has a way of touching that makes me feel wonderful. Generous." Now they were both watching her. "It's like love comes easily to her."

"God, you're romantic," his father said. "It must be your age."

"Want to hear about how wonderful she is? In bed?"

"No. No, I don't think so."

"You *used* to want to hear."

"I shouldn't've asked. That was a mistake. *Glückschmerz*. Besides, couples don't live in bed. You can't insult a waiter or cash a check in bed. As a paradigm for life, it's inadequate."

Eric was showing an unsteady smile. "I want to throw myself at her feet," he said. "We're the king and queen of lovers. Love. God, I just lap it up. We can go and go. I don't want life. I want love. And so does she."

"Have we always talked this way?" his father asked. "It's deplorable."

"We started getting a little raw about two years ago. That was when you began asking me about my girlfriends. Some pretty raw questions, things you shouldn't have been asking. I mean, we all know *why*, right?"

"Just looking out for my boy." In the cold, he could feel his eyelid twitching.

"You could mind your own business, Pop. You could try that." He said this with equanimity. Darlene was running back toward them. She ran awkwardly, with her upper torso leaning forward and her arms flailing. Three children were following her. As she panted, her breath was visible in the cold air.

"Sometimes I think I lead a strange life," Eric's father said. "Sometimes I think that none of this is real."

"Yeah, Chekhov," Eric said. "I read him, just like you told me to." Darlene ran straight up to Eric and put her blue mittens, which had bullet-sized balls of snow stuck to them, up to both sides of his face. She exposed all her teeth when she smiled. She took Eric's left hand. Then she reached down with her other hand and grasped Mr. Bradbury's doeskin glove. Standing between them, she said, "I love winter. I love the cold."

"Yes," Mr. Bradbury said. "The bitterness invigorates."

Not letting go of either of their hands, she walked between them back to the apartment building.

They sat around for the rest of the afternoon; Darlene tried to take a nap, and Eric and his father watched a basketball game, De Paul against Marquette. When the game was half over, Eric turned to his father and asked, "Where are your cigarettes, Pop?"

"My little friends? I evicted them."

"How come?"

"I quit in December. I woke up in the middle of the night

and thought I was fixing to die. The outlines of my heart were all but visible under the skin, it hurt so much. I felt like a corpse ready for the anatomy lesson. So: I stopped. Imagine this. I threw my gold Dunhill lighter, the one your mother gave me, down the building's trash shaft, along with all the cigarettes in the house. I heard the lighter whine and clatter all the way to the heap at the bottom. What a scarifying loss was there. And how I miss the nicotine. But I wasn't about to go. I may look like Samuel Gompers, but I'm only fifty-two. I figured there must be more to life than patient despair, right?"

Sitting on the floor, leaning against the sofa in which his father was sitting, Eric held his hand up in the air behind him. "Congratulations," he said. The two of them shook hands. "That took real guts."

"Thank you." He checked his fingers, still yellow from nicotine stains. "Yes, it did. I agree." He thumped his chest. "Guts."

At dinner Darlene was gulping her wine. "I don't get to drink this much at home. And furthermore, I shouldn't. Wine keeps you awake. Did you know that? What is this, French?" She peered at the label. "Romanian. Well. That was my next guess."

"A nice table wine," Mr. Bradbury said. "And when it turns, you can use it as salad dressing."

She looked at Eric. Eric shook his head, shrugged, and continued eating.

"He never says much at dinner," Darlene said, pointing at Eric. Mr. Bradbury nodded. After a pause, she said, "I don't think I ever told you about the time I met Bill Cosby."

At one o'clock Mr. Bradbury found himself lying awake, staring at the curtains. His back itched, and as he rubbed his neck he thought he felt a swelling. The damnable Romanian wine had given him a headache. Sitting up, he lowered his feet to the floor and put on his slippers. Then, shuffling across the bedroom, he opened the door that led out to the hallway.

He was halfway to the kitchen when he stopped outside Eric's bedroom door. He heard whispering. He stood and listened. It wasn't whispering so much as a drone from his son. "'The only completely stationary object in the room,'" he was saying, "'was an enormous couch on which two young women were buoyed up as though upon an anchored balloon.'" As Eric went on—Daisy and Tom and Jordan Baker undramatically droned into existence—his voice, indifferent to the story, spread out its soporific waves of narration. His father turned around and padded back into his own bedroom.

Three hours later, still feeling sleepless, Mr. Bradbury rose again out of bed and again advanced down the hall. All the lights were blazing. Halfway to the kitchen, he looked toward the refrigerator and saw the two of them huddled together side by side at the dining-room table, Darlene in her bathrobe, Eric in a nightshirt. Randomly he noticed the width of his son's shoulders, the fullness of Darlene's breasts. Her head was in her hands. Unobserved, Mr. Bradbury watched his son butter the bread, apply the mayonnaise, add the sandwich meat and the lettuce, close the sandwich, cut it in half, remove the crusts, and then hand it on its plate to her. "Thank you," she said. She began to eat. She chewed with her mouth open. She said, "You're so sweet. I love you." She kissed the air in his direction. Mr. Bradbury moved back, stood still, then turned toward his bedroom.

He closed the door and clicked on the bedside lamp. From far down on the other side of the hallway, he heard Darlene's loud laugh. He started to slip in under the covers, thought better of it, and went to his window to part the curtains. Getting back into bed, he switched off the bulb; then, with his head on the pillow, he gazed at the city skyline, half-consciously counting the few apartments in the high-rise across the street that still had all their lights burning.

Gryphon

➤⬧

On Wednesday afternoon, between the geography lesson on ancient Egypt's hand-operated irrigation system and an art project that involved drawing a model city next to a mountain, our fourth-grade teacher, Mr. Hibler, developed a cough. This cough began with a series of muffled throat-clearings and progressed to propulsive noises contained within Mr. Hibler's closed mouth. "Listen to him," Carol Peterson whispered to me. "He's gonna blow up." Mr. Hibler's laughter—dazed and infrequent—sounded a bit like his cough, but as we worked on our model cities we would look up, thinking he was enjoying a joke, and see Mr. Hibler's face turning red, his cheeks puffed out. This was not laughter. Twice he bent over, and his loose tie, like a plumb line, hung down straight from his neck as he exploded himself into a Kleenex. He would excuse himself, then go on coughing. "I'll bet you a dime," Carol Peterson whispered, "we get a substitute tomorrow."

Carol sat at the desk in front of mine and was a bad person—when she thought no one was looking she would blow her nose on notebook paper, then crumple it up and throw it into the wastebasket—but at times of crisis she spoke the truth. I knew I'd lose the dime.

"No deal," I said.

When Mr. Hibler stood us in formation at the door just prior to the final bell, he was almost incapable of speech. "I'm sorry, boys and girls," he said. "I seem to be coming down with something."

"I hope you feel better tomorrow, Mr. Hibler," Bobby Kryzanowicz, the faultless brown-noser, said, and I heard Carol Peterson's evil giggle. Then Mr. Hibler opened the door and we walked out to the buses, a clique of us starting noisily to hawk and raugh as soon as we thought we were a few feet beyond Mr. Hibler's earshot.

Since Five Oaks was a rural community, and in Michigan, the supply of substitute teachers was limited to the town's unemployed community college graduates, a pool of about four mothers. These ladies fluttered, provided easeful class days, and nervously covered material we had mastered weeks earlier. Therefore it was a surprise when a woman we had never seen came into the class the next day, carrying a purple purse, a checkerboard lunchbox, and a few books. She put the books on one side of Mr. Hibler's desk and the lunchbox on the other, next to the Voice of Music phonograph. Three of us in the back of the room were playing with Heever, the chameleon that lived in a terrarium and on one of the plastic drapes, when she walked in.

She clapped her hands at us. "Little boys," she said, "why are you bent over together like that?" She didn't wait for us to answer. "Are you tormenting an animal? Put it back. Please sit down at your desks. I want no cabals this time of the day." We just stared at her. "Boys," she repeated, "I asked you to sit down."

I put the chameleon in his terrarium and felt my way to my desk, never taking my eyes off the woman. With white and green chalk, she had started to draw a tree on the left side of the blackboard. She didn't look usual. Furthermore, her tree was outsized, disproportionate, for some reason.

"This room needs a tree," she said, with one line drawing the suggestion of a leaf. "A large, leafy, shady, deciduous . . . oak."

Her fine, light hair had been done up in what I would learn years later was called a chignon, and she wore gold-rimmed glasses whose lenses seemed to have the faintest blue tint. Harold Knardahl, who sat across from me, whispered, "Mars," and I nodded slowly, savoring the imminent weirdness of the day. The substitute drew another branch with an extravagant arm gesture, then turned around and said, "Good morning. I don't believe I said good morning to all of you yet."

Facing us, she was no special age—an adult is an adult—but her face had two prominent lines, descending vertically from the sides of her mouth to her chin. I knew where I had seen those lines before: *Pinocchio*. They were marionette lines. "You may stare at me," she said to us, as a few more kids from the last bus came into the room, their eyes fixed on her, "for a few more seconds, until the bell rings. Then I will permit no more staring. Looking I will permit. Staring, no. It is impolite to stare, and a sign of bad breeding. You cannot make a social effort while staring."

Harold Knardahl did not glance at me, or nudge, but I heard him whisper "Mars" again, trying to get more mileage out of his single joke with the kids who had just come in.

When everyone was seated, the substitute teacher finished her tree, put down her chalk fastidiously on the phonograph, brushed her hands, and faced us. "Good morning," she said. "I am Miss Ferenczi, your teacher for the day. I am fairly new to your community, and I don't believe any of you know me. I will therefore start by telling you a story about myself."

While we settled back, she launched into her tale. She said her grandfather had been a Hungarian prince; her mother had been born in some place called Flanders, had been a pianist, and had played concerts for people Miss Ferenczi referred to as "crowned heads." She gave us a knowing look. "Grieg," she said, "the Norwegian master, wrote a concerto for piano that was . . . "—she paused—"my mother's triumph at her debut concert in London." Her eyes searched the ceiling. Our eyes followed. Nothing up there but ceiling tile. "For reasons that I shall not go into, my family's fortunes took us to Detroit, then north to dreadful Saginaw, and now here I am in Five Oaks, as your substitute teacher, for today, Thursday, October the eleventh. I believe it will be a good day: all the forecasts coincide. We shall start with your reading lesson. Take out your reading book. I believe it is called *Broad Horizons*, or something along those lines."

Jeannie Vermeesch raised her hand. Miss Ferenczi nodded at her. "Mr. Hibler always starts the day with the Pledge of Allegiance," Jeannie whined.

"Oh, does he? In that case," Miss Ferenczi said, "you must know it *very* well by now, and we certainly need not spend our time on it. No, no allegiance pledging on the premises today, by my reckoning. Not with so much sunlight coming into the room. A pledge does not suit my mood." She glanced at her watch. "Time *is* flying. Take out *Broad Horizons*."

She disappointed us by giving us an ordinary lesson, complete with vocabulary and drills, comprehension questions, and recitation. She didn't seem to care for the material, however. She sighed every few minutes and rubbed her glasses with a frilly handkerchief that she withdrew, magician-style, from her left sleeve.

After reading we moved on to arithmetic. It was my favorite time of the morning, when the lazy autumn sunlight dazzled its way through ribbons of clouds past the windows on the east side of the classroom and crept across the linoleum floor. On the playground the first group of children, the kindergartners, were running on the quack grass just beyond the monkey bars. We were doing multiplication tables. Miss Ferenczi had made John Wazny stand up at his desk in the front row. He was supposed to go through the tables of six. From where I was sitting, I could smell the Vitalis soaked into John's plastered hair. He was doing fine until he came to six times eleven and six times twelve. "Six times eleven," he said, "is sixty-eight. Six times twelve is . . . " He put his fingers to his head, quickly and secretly sniffed his fingertips, and said, " . . . seventy-two." Then he sat down.

"Fine," Miss Ferenczi said. "Well now. That was very good."

"Miss Ferenczi!" One of the Eddy twins was waving her hand desperately in the air. "Miss Ferenczi! Miss Ferenczi!"

"Yes?"

"John said that six times eleven is sixty-eight and you said he was right!"

"*Did* I?" She gazed at the class with a jolly look breaking across her marionette's face. "Did I say that? Well, what *is* six times eleven?"

"It's sixty-six!"

She nodded. "Yes. So it is. But, and I know some people will not entirely agree with me, at some times it is sixty-eight."

"When? When is it sixty-eight?"

We were all waiting.

"In higher mathematics, which you children do not yet understand, six times eleven can be considered to be sixty-eight." She laughed through her nose. "In higher mathematics numbers are . . . more fluid. The only thing a number does is contain a certain amount of something. Think of water. A cup is not the only way to measure a certain amount of water, is it?" We were staring, shaking our heads. "You could use saucepans or thimbles. In either case, the water *would be the same.* Perhaps," she started again, "it would be better for you to think that six times eleven is sixty-eight only when I am in the room."

"Why is it sixty-eight," Mark Poole asked, "when you're in the room?"

"Because it's more interesting that way," she said, smiling very rapidly behind her blue-tinted glasses. "Besides, I'm your substitute teacher, am I not?" We all nodded. "Well, then, think of six times eleven equals sixty-eight as a substitute fact."

"A substitute fact?"

"Yes." Then she looked at us carefully. "Do you think," she

asked, "that anyone is going to be hurt by a substitute fact?"

We looked back at her.

"Will the plants on the windowsill be hurt?" We glanced at them. There were sensitive plants thriving in a green plastic tray, and several wilted ferns in small clay pots. "Your dogs and cats, or your moms and dads?" She waited. "So," she concluded, "what's the problem?"

"But it's wrong," Janice Weber said, "isn't it?"

"What's your name, young lady?"

"Janice Weber."

"And you think it's wrong, Janice?"

"I was just asking."

"Well, all right. You were just asking. I think we've spent enough time on this matter by now, don't you, class? You are free to think what you like. When your teacher, Mr. Hibler, returns, six times eleven will be sixty-six again, you can rest assured. And it will be that for the rest of your lives in Five Oaks. Too bad, eh?" She raised her eyebrows and glinted herself at us. "But for now, it wasn't. So much for that. Let us go on to your assigned problems for today, as painstakingly outlined, I see, in Mr. Hibler's lesson plan. Take out a sheet of paper and write your names on the upper left-hand corner."

For the next half hour we did the rest of our arithmetic problems. We handed them in and then went on to spelling, my worst subject. Spelling always came before lunch. We were taking spelling dictation and looking at the clock. "Thorough," Miss Ferenczi said. "Boundary." She walked in the aisles between the desks, holding the spelling book open and looking down at our papers. "Balcony." I clutched my pencil. Somehow, the way she said those words, they seemed foreign, mis-voweled and mis-consonanted. I stared down at what I had spelled. *Balconie*. I turned the pencil upside down and erased my mistake. *Balconey*. That looked better, but still incorrect. I cursed the world of spelling and tried erasing it again and saw the paper beginning to wear away. *Balkony*. Suddenly I felt a hand on my shoulder.

"I don't like that word either," Miss Ferenczi whispered, bent over, her mouth near my ear. "It's ugly. My feeling is, if you don't like a word, you don't have to use it." She straightened up, leaving behind a slight odor of Clorets.

At lunchtime we went out to get our trays of sloppy joes, peaches in heavy syrup, coconut cookies, and milk, and brought them back to the classroom, where Miss Ferenczi was sitting at the desk, eating a brown sticky thing she had unwrapped from tightly rubber-banded waxed paper. "Miss Ferenczi," I said, raising my hand. "You don't have to eat with us. You can eat with the other teachers. There's a teacher's lounge," I ended up, "next to the principal's office."

"No, thank you," she said. "I prefer it here."

"We've got a room monitor," I said. "Mrs. Eddy." I pointed to where Mrs. Eddy, Joyce and Judy's mother, sat silently at the back of the room, doing her knitting.

"That's fine," Miss Ferenczi said. "But I shall continue to eat here, with you children. I prefer it," she repeated.

"How come?" Wayne Razmer asked without raising his hand.

"I talked to the other teachers before class this morning," Miss Ferenczi said, biting into her brown food. "There was a great rattling of the words for the fewness of the ideas. I didn't care for their brand of hilarity. I don't like ditto-machine jokes."

"Oh," Wayne said.

"What's that you're eating?" Maxine Sylvester asked, twitching her nose. "Is it food?"

"It most certainly *is* food. It's a stuffed fig. I had to drive almost down to Detroit to get it. I also brought some smoked sturgeon. And this," she said, lifting some green leaves out of her lunchbox, "is raw spinach, cleaned this morning."

"Why're you eating raw spinach?" Maxine asked.

"It's good for you," Miss Ferenczi said. "More stimulating than soda pop or smelling salts." I bit into my sloppy joe and stared blankly out the window. An almost invisible moon was faintly silvered in the daytime autumn sky. "As far as food is concerned," Miss Ferenczi was saying, "you have to shuffle the pack. Mix it up. Too many people eat . . . well, never mind."

"Miss Ferenczi," Carol Peterson said, "what are we going to do this afternoon?"

"Well," she said, looking down at Mr. Hibler's lesson plan, "I see that your teacher, Mr. Hibler, has you scheduled for a unit on the Egyptians." Carol groaned. "Yessss," Miss Ferenczi continued, "that is what we will do: the Egyptians. A remarkable people. Almost as remarkable as the Americans. But not quite." She lowered her head, did her quick smile, and went back to eating her spinach.

After noon recess we came back into the classroom and saw that Miss Ferenczi had drawn a pyramid on the blackboard close to her oak tree. Some of us who had been playing baseball were messing around in the back of the room, dropping the bats and gloves into the playground box, and Ray Schontzeler had just slugged me when I heard Miss Ferenczi's high-pitched voice, quavering with emotions. "Boys," she said, "come to order right this minute and take your seats. I do not wish to waste a minute of class time. Take out your geography books." We trudged to our desks and, still sweating, pulled out *Distant Lands and Their People*. "Turn to page forty-two." She waited for thirty seconds, then looked over at Kelly Munger. "Young man," she said, "why are you still fossicking in your desk?"

Kelly looked as if his foot had been stepped on. "Why am I what?"

"Why are you . . . burrowing in your desk like that?"

"I'm lookin' for the book, Miss Ferenczi."

Bobby Kryzanowicz, the faultless brown-noser who sat in the first row by choice, softly said, "His name is Kelly Munger. He can't ever find his stuff. He always does that."

"I don't care what his name is, especially after lunch," Miss Ferenczi said. *"Where is your book?"*

"I just found it." Kelly was peering into his desk and with both hands pulled at the book, shoveling along in front of it several pencils and crayons, which fell into his lap and then to the floor.

"I hate a mess," Miss Ferenczi said. "I hate a mess in a desk or a mind. It's . . . unsanitary. You wouldn't want your house at home to look like your desk at school, now, would you?" She didn't wait for an answer. "I should think not. A house at home should be as neat as human hands can make it. What were we talking about? Egypt. Page forty-two. I note from Mr. Hibler's lesson plan that you have been discussing the modes of Egyptian irrigation. Interesting, in my view, but not so interesting as what we are about to cover. The pyramids, and Egyptian slave labor. A plus on one side, a minus on the other." We had our books open to page forty-two, where there was a picture of a pyramid, but Miss Ferenczi wasn't looking at the book. Instead, she was staring at some object just outside the window.

"Pyramids," Miss Ferenczi said, still looking past the window. "I want you to think about pyramids. And what was inside. The bodies of the pharaohs, of course, and their attendant treasures. Scrolls. Perhaps," Miss Ferenczi said, her face gleeful but unsmiling, "these scrolls were novels for the pharaohs, helping them to pass the time in their long voyage through the centuries. But then, I am joking." I was looking at the lines on Miss Ferenczi's skin. "Pyramids," Miss Ferenczi went on, "were the repositories of special cosmic powers. The nature of a pyramid is to guide cosmic energy forces into a concentrated point. The Egyptians knew that; we have generally forgotten it. Did you know," she asked, walking to the side of the room so that she was standing by the coat closet, "that George Washington had Egyptian blood, from his grandmother? Certain features of the Constitution of the United States are notable for their Egyptian ideas."

Without glancing down at the book, she began to talk about the movement of souls in Egyptian religion. She said that when people die, their souls return to Earth in the form of carpenter ants or walnut trees, depending on how they behaved—"well or ill"—in life. She said that the Egyptians believed that people act the way they do because of magnetism produced by tidal forces in the solar system, forces produced by the sun and by its "planetary ally," Jupiter. Jupiter, she said, was a planet, as we had been told, but had "certain properties of stars." She was speaking very fast. She said that the Egyptians were great explorers and conquerors. She said that the greatest of all the conquerors, Genghis Khan, had had forty horses and forty young women killed on the site of his grave. We listened. No one tried to stop her. "I myself have been in Egypt," she said, "and have witnessed much dust and many brutalities." She said that an old man in Egypt who worked for a circus had personally shown her an animal in a cage, a monster, half bird and half lion. She said that this monster was called a gryphon and that she had heard about them but never seen them until she traveled to the outskirts of Cairo. She wrote the word out on the blackboard in large capital letters: GRYPHON. She said that Egyptian astronomers had discovered the planet Saturn but had not seen its rings. She said that the Egyptians were the first to discover that dogs, when they are ill, will not drink from rivers, but wait for rain, and hold their jaws open to catch it.

"She lies."

We were on the school bus home. I was sitting next to Carl Whiteside, who had bad breath and a huge collection of marbles. We were arguing. Carl thought she was lying. I said she wasn't, probably.

"I didn't believe that stuff about the bird," Carl said, "and what she told us about the pyramids? I didn't believe that, either. She didn't know what she was talking about."

"Oh yeah?" I had liked her. She was strange. I thought I could nail him. "If she was lying," I said, "what'd she say that was a lie?"

"Six times eleven isn't sixty-eight. It isn't ever. It's sixty-six, I know for a fact."

"She said so. She admitted it. What else did she lie about?"

"I don't know," he said. "Stuff."

"What stuff?"

"Well." He swung his legs back and forth. "You ever see an animal that was half lion and half bird?" He crossed his arms. "It sounded real fakey to me."

"It could happen," I said. I had to improvise, to outrage him. "I read in this newspaper my mom bought in the IGA about this scientist, this mad scientist in the Swiss Alps, and he's been putting genes and chromosomes and stuff together in test tubes, and he combined a human being and a hamster." I waited, for effect. "It's called a humster."

"You never." Carl was staring at me, his mouth open, his terrible bad breath making its way toward me. "What newspaper was it?"

"*The National Enquirer,*" I said, "that they sell next to the cash registers." When I saw his look of recognition, I knew I had him. "And this mad scientist," I said, "his name was, um, Dr. Frankenbush." I realized belatedly that this name was a mistake and waited for Carl to notice its resemblance to the name of the other famous mad master of permutations, but he only sat there.

"A man and a hamster?" He was staring at me, squinting, his mouth opening in distaste. "Jeez. What'd it look like?"

When the bus reached my stop, I took off down our dirt road and ran up through the backyard, kicking the tire swing for good luck. I dropped my books on the back steps so I could hug and kiss our dog, Mr. Selby. Then I hurried inside. I could smell brussels sprouts cooking, my unfavorite vegetable. My mother was washing other vegetables in the kitchen sink, and my baby brother was hollering in his yellow playpen on the kitchen floor.

"Hi, Mom," I said, hopping around the playpen to kiss her. "Guess what?"

"I have no idea."

"We had this substitute today, Miss Ferenczi, and I'd never seen her before, and she had all these stories and ideas and stuff."

"Well. That's good." My mother looked out the window in front of the sink, her eyes on the pine woods west of our house. That time of the afternoon her skin always looked so white to me. Strangers always said my mother looked like Betty Crocker, framed by the giant spoon on the side of the Bisquick box. "Listen, Tommy," she said. "Would you please go upstairs and pick your clothes off the floor in the bathroom, and then go outside to the shed and put the shovel and ax away that your father left outside this morning?"

"She said that six times eleven was sometimes sixty-eight!" I said. "And she said she once saw a monster that was half lion and half bird." I waited. "In Egypt."

"Did you hear me?" my mother asked, raising her arm to wipe her forehead with the back of her hand. "You have chores to do."

"I know," I said. "I was just telling you about the substitute."

"It's very interesting," my mother said, quickly glancing down at me, "and we can talk about it later when your father gets home. But right now you have some work to do."

"Okay, Mom." I took a cookie out of the jar on the counter and was about to go outside when I had a thought. I ran into the living room, pulled out a dictionary next to the TV stand, and opened it to the Gs. After five minutes I found it. *Gryphon*: variant of griffin. *Griffin*: "a fabulous beast with the head and wings of an eagle and the body of a lion." Fabulous was right. I shouted with triumph and ran outside to put my father's tools in their proper places.

Miss Ferenczi was back the next day, slightly altered. She had pulled her hair down and twisted it into pigtails, with red rubber bands holding them tight one inch from the ends. She was wearing a green blouse and pink scarf, making her difficult to look at for a full class day. This time there was no pretense of doing a reading lesson or moving on to arithmetic. As soon as the bell rang, she simply began to talk.

She talked for forty minutes straight. There seemed to be less connection between her ideas, but the ideas themselves were, as the dictionary would say, fabulous. She said she had heard of a huge jewel, in what she called the antipodes, that was so brilliant that when light shone into it at a certain angle it would blind whoever was looking at its center. She said the biggest diamond in the world was cursed and had killed everyone who owned it, and that by a trick of fate it was called the Hope Diamond. Diamonds are magic, she said, and this is why women wear them on their fingers, as a sign of the magic of womanhood. Men have strength, Miss Ferenczi said, but no true magic. That is why men fall in love with women but women do not fall in love with men: they just love being loved. George Washington had died because of a mistake he made about a diamond. Washington was not the first *true* President, but she didn't say who was. In some places in the world, she said, men and women still live in the trees and eat monkeys for breakfast. Their doctors are magicians. At the bottom of the sea are creatures thin as pancakes who have never been studied by scientists because when you take them up to air, the fish explode.

There was not a sound in the classroom, except for Miss

Ferenczi's voice, and Donna DeShano's coughing. No one even went to the bathroom.

Beethoven, she said, had not been deaf; it was a trick to make himself famous, and it worked. As she talked, Miss Ferenczi's pigtails swung back and forth. There are trees in the world, she said, that eat meat: their leaves are sticky and close up on bugs like hands. She lifted her hands and brought them together, palm to palm. Venus, which most people think is the next closest planet to the sun, is not always closer, and, besides, it is the planet of greatest mystery because of its thick cloud cover. "I know what lies underneath those clouds," Miss Ferenczi said, and waited. After the silence, she said, "Angels. Angels live under those clouds." She said that angels were not invisible to everyone and were in fact smarter than most people. They did not dress in robes as was often claimed but instead wore formal evening clothes, as if they were about to attend a concert. Often angels *do* attend concerts and sit in the aisles, where, she said, most people pay no attention to them. She said the most terrible angel had the shape of the Sphinx. "There is no running away from that one," she said. She said that unquenchable fires burn just under the surface of the earth in Ohio, and that the baby Mozart fainted dead away in his cradle when he first heard the sound of a trumpet. She said that someone named Narzim al Harrardim was the greatest writer who ever lived. She said that planets control behavior, and anyone conceived during a solar eclipse would be born with webbed feet.

"I know you children like to hear these things," she said, "these secrets, and that is why I am telling you all this." We nodded. It was better than doing comprehension questions for the readings in *Broad Horizons*.

"I will tell you one more story," she said, "and then we will have to do arithmetic." She leaned over, and her voice grew soft. "There is no death," she said. "You must never be afraid.

Never. That which is, cannot die. It will change into different earthly and unearthly elements, but I know this as sure as I stand here in front of you, and I swear it: you must not be afraid. I have seen this truth with these eyes. I know it because in a dream God kissed me. Here." And she pointed with her right index finger to the side of her head, below the mouth where the vertical lines were carved into her skin.

Absentmindedly we all did our arithmetic problems. At recess the class was out on the playground, but no one was playing. We were all standing in small groups, talking about Miss Ferenczi. We didn't know if she was crazy, or what. I looked out beyond the playground, at the rusted cars piled in a small heap behind a clump of sumac, and I wanted to see shapes there, approaching me.

On the way home, Carl sat next to me again. He didn't say much, and I didn't either. At last he turned to me. "You know what she said about the leaves that close up on bugs?"

"Huh?"

"The leaves," Carl insisted. "The meat-eating plants. I know it's true. I saw it on television. The leaves have this icky glue that the plants have got smeared all over them and the insects can't get off 'cause they're stuck. I saw it." He seemed demoralized. "She's tellin' the truth."

"Yeah."

"You think she's seen all those angels?"

I shrugged.

"I don't think she has," Carl informed me. "I think she made that part up."

"There's a tree," I suddenly said. I was looking out the window at the farms along County Road H. I knew every barn, every broken windmill, every fence, every anhydrous ammonia tank, by heart. "There's a tree that's . . . that I've seen . . . "

"Don't you try to do it," Carl said. "You'll just sound like a jerk."

I kissed my mother. She was standing in front of the stove. "How was your day?" she asked.

"Fine."

"Did you have Miss Ferenczi again?"

"Yeah."

"Well?"

"She was fine. Mom," I asked, "can I go to my room?"

"No," she said, "not until you've gone out to the vegetable garden and picked me a few tomatoes." She glanced at the sky. "I think it's going to rain. Skedaddle and do it now. Then you come back inside and watch your brother for a few minutes while I go upstairs. I need to clean up before dinner." She looked down at me. "You're looking a little pale, Tommy." She touched the back of her hand to my forehead and I felt her diamond ring against my skin. "Do you feel all right?"

"I'm fine," I said, and went out to pick the tomatoes.

Coughing mutedly, Mr. Hibler was back the next day, slipping lozenges into his mouth when his back was turned at forty-five-minute intervals and asking us how much of his prepared lesson plan Miss Ferenczi had followed. Edith Atwater took the responsibility for the class of explaining to Mr. Hibler that the substitute hadn't always done exactly what he, Mr. Hibler, would have done, but we had worked hard even though she talked a lot. About what? he asked. All kinds of things, Edith said. I sort of forgot. To our relief, Mr. Hibler seemed not at all interested in what Miss Ferenczi had said to fill the day. He probably thought it was woman's talk: unserious and not suited for school. It was enough that he had a pile of arithmetic problems from us to correct.

For the next month, the sumac turned a distracting red in

the field, and the sun traveled toward the southern sky, so that its rays reached Mr. Hibler's Halloween display on the bulletin board in the back of the room, fading the pumpkin head scarecrow from orange to tan. Every three days I measured how much farther the sun had moved toward the southern horizon by making small marks with my black Crayola on the north wall, ant-sized marks only I knew were there.

And then in early December, four days after the first permanent snowfall, she appeared again in our classroom. The minute she came in the door, I felt my heart begin to pound. Once again, she was different: this time, her hair hung straight down and seemed hardly to have been combed. She hadn't brought her lunchbox with her, but she was carrying what seemed to be a small box. She greeted all of us and talked about the weather. Donna DeShano had to remind her to take her overcoat off.

When the bell to start the day finally rang, Miss Ferenczi looked out at all of us and said, "Children, I have enjoyed your company in the past, and today I am going to reward you." She held up the small box. "Do you know what this is?" She waited. "Of course you don't. It is a Tarot pack."

Edith Atwater raised her hand. "What's a Tarot pack, Miss Ferenczi?"

"It is used to tell fortunes," she said. "And that is what I shall do this morning. I shall tell your fortunes, as I have been taught to do."

"What's fortune?" Bobby Kryzanowicz asked.

"The future, young man. I shall tell you what your future will be. I can't do your whole future, of course. I shall have to limit myself to the five-card system, the wands, cups, swords, pentacles, and the higher arcanes. Now who wants to be first?"

There was a long silence. Then Carol Peterson raised her hand.

"All right," Miss Ferenczi said. She divided the pack into

five smaller packs and walked back to Carol's desk, in front of mine. "Pick one card from each one of these packs," she said. I saw that Carol had a four of cups and a six of swords, but I couldn't see the other cards. Miss Ferenczi studied the cards on Carol's desk for a minute. "Not bad," she said. "I do not see much higher education. Probably an early marriage. Many children. There's something bleak and dreary here, but I can't tell what. Perhaps just the tasks of a housewife life. I think you'll do very well, for the most part." She smiled at Carol, a smile with a certain lack of interest. "Who wants to be next?"

Carl Whiteside raised his hand slowly.

"Yes," Miss Ferenczi said, "let's do a boy." She walked over to where Carl sat. After he picked his five cards, she gazed at them for a long time. "Travel," she said. "Much distant travel. You might go into the army. Not too much romantic interest here. A late marriage, if at all. But the Sun in your major arcana, that's a very good card." She giggled. "You'll have a happy life."

Next I raised my hand. She told me my future. She did the same with Bobby Kryzanowicz, Kelly Munger, Edith Atwater, and Kim Foor. Then she came to Wayne Razmer. He picked his five cards, and I could see that the Death card was one of them.

"What's your name?" Miss Ferenczi asked.

"Wayne."

"Well, Wayne," she said, "you will undergo a great metamorphosis, a change, before you become an adult. Your earthly element will no doubt leap higher, because you seem to be a sweet boy. This card, this nine of swords, tells me of suffering and desolation. And this ten of wands, well, that's a heavy load."

"What about this one?" Wayne pointed at the Death card.

"It means, my sweet, that you will die soon." She gathered up the cards. We were all looking at Wayne. "But do not fear," she said. "It is not really death. Just change. Out of your earthly shape." She put the cards on Mr. Hibler's desk. "And now, let's do some arithmetic."

At lunchtime Wayne went to Mr. Faegre, the principal, and informed him of what Miss Ferenczi had done. During the noon recess, we saw Miss Ferenczi drive out of the parking lot in her rusting green Rambler American. I stood under the slide, listening to the other kids coasting down and landing in the little depressive bowls at the bottom. I was kicking stones and tugging at my hair right up to the moment when I saw Wayne come out to the playground. He smiled, the dead fool, and with the fingers of his right hand he was showing everyone how he had told on Miss Ferenczi.

I made my way toward Wayne, pushing myself past two girls from another class. He was watching me with his little pinhead eyes.

"You told," I shouted at him. "She was just kidding."

"She shouldn't have," he shouted back. "We were supposed to be doing arithmetic."

"She just scared you," I said. "You're a chicken. You're a chicken, Wayne. You are. Scared of a little card," I sing-songed.

Wayne fell at me, his two fists hammering down on my nose. I gave him a good one in the stomach and then I tried for his head. Aiming my fist, I saw that he was crying. I slugged him.

"She was right," I yelled. "She was always right! She told the truth!" Other kids were whooping. "You were just scared, that's all!"

And then large hands pulled at us, and it was my turn to speak to Mr. Faegre.

In the afternoon Miss Ferenczi was gone, and my nose was stuffed with cotton clotted with blood, and my lip had swelled, and our class had been combined with Mrs. Mantei's sixth-grade class for a crowded afternoon science unit on insect life in ditches and swamps. I knew where Mrs. Mantei lived: she had a new house trailer just down the road from us, at the Clearwater Park. She was no mystery. Somehow she and Mr. Bodine, the other fourth-grade teacher, had managed to fit forty-five desks into the room. Kelly Munger asked if Miss Ferenczi had been arrested, and Mrs. Mantei said no, of course not. All that afternoon, until the buses came to pick us up, we learned about field crickets and two-striped grasshoppers, water bugs, cicadas, mosquitoes, flies, and moths. We learned about insects' hard outer shell, the exoskeleton, and the usual parts of the mouth, including the labrum, mandible, maxilla, and glossa. We learned about compound eyes, and the four-stage metamorphosis from egg to larva to pupa to adult. We learned something, but not much, about mating. Mrs. Mantei drew, very skillfully, the internal anatomy of the grasshopper on the blackboard. We learned about the dance of the honeybee, directing other bees in the hive to pollen. We found out about which insects were pests to man, and which were not. On lined white pieces of paper we made lists of insects we might actually see, then a list of insects too small to be clearly visible, such as fleas; Mrs. Mantei said that our assignment would be to memorize these lists for the next day, when Mr. Hibler would certainly return and test us on our knowledge.

Through the Safety Net

✦

D r. Nadler, the dentist, was eating the sole amandine luncheon plate at La Maison Blanche when she was paged.

"The psychic called," her husband said. "He says for you to call him right back, the next half hour. He has some errands to run this afternoon and won't be reachable after one o'clock. Same with me. I gotta go. See you tonight. Bye."

She asked how to make an outgoing call. She dialed nine first, as instructed, then the psychic's number. "This is Dinah Nadler," she said when he answered. "What's up?"

"We need to make an appointment," the psychic said. Then he blew his nose, making an odd sound, a long wet snort. "Excuse me," he said, "but it's just a cold. One of those sinus colds that started as an ear cold. My nephews were in last week from Boston with their mother, and they all brought these little coughs and sneezes with them. Cute but contagious. Well. What about this afternoon? It's important."

"Busy," she said. "I have appointments."

"How about tomorrow?"

"Four o'clock," she told him. "Not a minute earlier."

"Fine," the psychic said. His name was Herbert. "I'll be here, ready and waiting."

At four-fifteen she knocked at the psychic's apartment, which also served as his office. "Come in," he said.

"How's the cold?" she asked. She sat down in a shabby dark-blue overstuffed chair. She looked at the two pictures on the wall, one of a woodland stream, the other of a watermill, and immediately felt depressed.

The psychic's nose was red from postnasal drip. "It's getting better," he said. "I'll be over it by tomorrow. How are you, Dinah? You're looking well."

"I've been busy," she said, stroking her forehead. "This afternoon, an impacted wisdom tooth—"

"Please," the psychic said, holding up his hand. "No details. Dentistry doesn't inspire me." He frowned. In Southfield, north of Detroit, there were two psychics acknowledged to be accurate; this one, Herbert, was the younger. He was just starting out and was in his early thirties, but he had the darkened, somewhat arresting look of a man who has fought and won in a battle with schizophrenia. Under no circumstances did he ever make eye contact.

"So," Dinah said, "what's new?"

"The good news first. Buy Michigan Consolidated Edison," the psychic said. "It's shamefully undervalued and it's going to go straight up. There's going to be a merger, a reorganization . . . something, I don't know exactly what. The Amalgamated is going to snatch it up. Okay. Next. Sell that little tool-and-die company you've been buying over the counter. That's a one-way ticket to nowhere, that company."

"Herbert," she said, "you're confused. My husband bought that. It's in his portfolio, not mine."

"A slight mistake," the psychic said. "How's your daughter? She must be . . . what? Three?"

"Four. She's fine. She's in nursery school. Is that why you called?"

"No."

"Why did you?"

"Yesterday morning I got a terrible feeling about you. What are you doing?"

"What do you mean, what am I doing?"

"It's a simple question." He blew his nose. "Comprehensible. What are you doing?"

"I'm doing," she said, "what I always do. I get up, I go to work, I go home."

"Oh no," the psychic said, putting his handkerchief away. "That's not the story. That's not the black spot on the horizon. We have another story here. That's definite. Are you planning a trip?"

"Not until next summer."

"You and Jake, are you in the market for a new house?"

"No."

"It's a black spot, Dinah. There it is, blinking, at the horizon, a blinking black spot. I just wish I could be more specific. I don't get messages like this every day. Your daughter . . . Sarah?"

"Sally," she corrected him.

"Sally." He sneezed. "Is she all right?"

"Fine. Just as I told you. Fine."

"Dinah, I don't want to be indelicate. You and Jake. Are you happy? I don't mean to pry."

"Of course it's prying," she told him. "We're very happy."

"Something's wrong," Herbert said. "Something is wrong with me or with you. It's not that dog of yours, is it? That Weimaraner?"

"Otto."

"Yes, Otto."

"Otto is fine."

"Then I don't know what's the matter with me."

"What did you see?" Dinah asked.

"Calamity," the psychic said. "Not to mince words."

"What kind of calamity?" Dinah asked, jarred.

"What kind? The Book of Job kind. I saw your whole life, your house, car, that swimming pool you put in last summer, the career, your child, and the whole future just start to radiate with this ugly black flame from the inside, poof, and then I saw you falling, like at the circus, down from the trapeze. Whoops, and down, and then through the safety net. Through the ground."

Dinah made a sound in her throat.

"Yes," the psychic said, "that's how I feel too. And after all this work, too, these years of dedication. I can't get it more specific yet. I'm not pulling the specifics in on my antenna. I'm not getting that station. Please don't go out to the backyard and start chopping down trees. Don't try to get a pilot's license. Be careful in your work."

"I *am* careful in my work," Dinah said.

"All this makes me nervous," the psychic said. "I usually have these things in better focus." He got up and scratched his scalp. Dinah noticed food stains on his corduroy trousers.

"I wish you'd change the pictures on the wall," she said.

"My mother gave me that one," he said, pointing at the babbling brook. "I bought the other one at K-Mart, to match it."

"Well," Jake said at dinner, "what did Herbert say?"

She put down her glass of wine, a 1976 Liberty School cabernet. "I wasn't going to tell you."

"That bad?"

"Worse. First he said to buy Consolidated Michigan Edison. Then he said, quote, calamity, unquote."

"What kind of calamity? Significant capital losses?"

"That's the catch. It's not the investments he's talking about. This is personal. He started asking me about our marriage, if you can believe it. Him asking me about our relationship was a scene out of a Bergman movie. Grotesque. Anyway, he said he didn't have anything in focus. We're not supposed to do anything risky, he says."

"We should stop going to that guy," Jake said. "He was always north Detroit wacko, but at least we used to make money off of him."

"Don't forget what he told us about Northeastern BankTel."

"I haven't forgotten."

"Up twenty points in five months."

"I remember. We paid for the swimming pool with that tip. I haven't forgotten Lincoln Tri-State Insurance, either."

She raised the crystal wineglass to him.

Dinah was drilling a first upper left bicuspid when the nurse came up behind her. "Call Herbert," she whispered. "He says he'll be in all afternoon."

Twenty minutes later Dinah was on the phone. "Well?"

"It's not you," the psychic said. "It must be Jake, your husband."

"What did you see?" Dinah asked.

"Picture this," the psychic said. "There's a field, and a tree, and the shape of this tree is *disgusting*. It's a disgusting tree, Dinah, I don't know how else to describe it, gnarled and burnt but with this awful blue fruit still growing on it, like blistered plums."

"What's this have to do with Jake?"

"It has something to do with Jake."

"What?"

"I don't know yet."

"Herbert," she said. "I think we'd better stop this. If you can't be specific, I don't think I want your help anymore. I can't use generalized catastrophes."

"I don't blame you," he said. "I don't know what's gone wrong with the signals."

That night, as she was putting her daugher to bed, she smelled the air for gas. In the cold Michigan winter night the wind blew against the side of the house and against the roof, underneath which, bedded between the slats of the attic, the

Corning fiberglass insulation held the warmth underneath and the cold above. As her daughter fell asleep, Dinah listened carefully to the rhythms of her child's breathing. She checked the room for sharp edges. Then she went downstairs, walked past her husband, asleep, mouth open, in the den, where he sat propped in front of the television set, Otto asleep next to him. In the kitchen she checked the burners on the stove. She went back into the den and shut off the VCR. Down by Jake's dangling left hand, on the tile floor, beside the rug, there was a water glass, not broken. Falling asleep, he had dropped it. Dinah went to fetch a few paper towels, and Otto watched her as she cleaned up.

She returned to the kitchen and sat down at the circular breakfast table. She folded both hands in front of her as she listened to the click of the quartz kitchen clock above the sink. Feeling hungry, she opened the refrigerator and picked out a grapefruit from a group of five gathered in the crisper. From a drawer to the left of the sink, she took a four-inch serrated knife. Holding the knife and the grapefruit in her left hand, she opened the cupboard and took out a green glass plate with her right hand. As she took out the plate, the knife slipped from her hand and fell to the floor, where it slid toward the stove. She reached down and picked it up. Against her palm the knife's handle felt smooth and cold.

She dimmed the light above the breakfast table with the rheostat switch and began to cut into the grapefruit with the serrated knife. Keeping her fingers out of the way, she sliced the grapefruit in half, then began to cut it into sections. She stood up again to get a spoon from the drawer. As she was sliding the drawer open, the doorbell rang.

She thought of Jake in the den, then shrugged her shoulders and went to the foyer. Without looking through the glass panels on either side of the door, she turned the lock. Standing behind the storm door was Gary Slominski, the paperboy, collecting. He wore a gray winter hat, army surplus overcoat, and brown boots. Dinah went to her purse in the front hall, on the first step of the stairs, took out six dollars, and went back to where Gary was standing on the stoop. "Thank you," he said as she handed the money to him.

She closed the door, locked it, and walked back into the kitchen. She sat down again under the light and absentmindedly began to eat the grapefruit she had already sliced. She heard the furnace going on, blowing heat into the four corners of the house. From the living room came the sound of something striking the picture window, perhaps a bird blown into the glass by the windstorm. She decided to wait to check on it until she had finished eating. Then she heard a similar sound: some object, again, striking the window. At almost the same moment, the phone began to ring. She stood up, dried her hands on a dishtowel, walked over to where it was hanging, and answered it.

"Hello," she said.

"It isn't Jake," the psychic said. "I was wrong about that."

"Herbert, you need a rest. Sun. Sun for your sinuses. I recommend Florida. You're going haywire."

"I know. This is my last call, almost. I've called everyone I know. I just wanted to tell you it's not Jake."

"Good," Dinah said. "I'm glad to hear that."

"It's everybody," he said, and hung up.

Dinah put back the phone on its cradle, looked at the ceiling, then sat down again and finished the grapefruit. She put the yellow rind into a brown paper bag in the garbage can under the sink, and she rinsed the dish and the knife and put them in the yellow plastic dish drainer. Then she walked into the living room and positioned herself in front of the picture window. She looked down at the lawn, lightly covered now with snow. Underneath the window she saw a sparrow with a broken wing pulling itself in half-circles around on the grass. Beyond the bird she saw their ash tree; something about its shape and color gave her a shock.

Then, like a horn of announcement, Otto set up a howl. This was followed by a steady roar of barking. Dinah looked up into the sky, then turned off all the lights on the side table next to the sofa behind her. Then she went back to the window, cupped her hands on both sides of her face, and looked outside to see what was happening.

A Late Sunday Afternoon
by the Huron

A modest place, Delhi Metropark stands 850 feet above sea level and is located six miles west of Ann Arbor, Michigan, along the Huron River. This river originates in Pontiac Lake to the north and flows into Lake Erie, eighty miles downstream. The latitude of this spot is 42 degrees, 52 minutes, 30 seconds, the longitude 83 degrees, 52 minutes, 30 seconds. On this particular day, Sunday morning in mid-June, the families begin to arrive at 10:25, stumbling out of their rusty station wagons crammed with bags of charcoal, food coolers, kids, dogs, and pieces of recreational plastic. The lovers, and those coming alone, will arrive later in the day; right now they are still lying in bed, sipping coffee from no-spill mugs, and staring toward the white muslin curtains. What sort of day is it? What's going to happen with the weather?

At 10:40 the temperature is 71 degrees Fahrenheit, the humidity 56 percent, the barometer 29.54 and falling slowly. The midmorning sky is flecked with cirrus clouds, fleecy lines of ice crystals twenty thousand feet overhead, often the vanguard of a low-pressure front. It might rain.

Among these early-arriving families a couple, holding hands at the fingertips, stands next to the water. They appear to be unmarried and in their early twenties. Now he is taking off his blue cotton jacket and dropping it on the grass; then he takes off his shoes and socks and rolls up his cotton trouser cuffs. She removes a light-pink sweater and puts her hand in the small of his back for balance when she unlaces her running shoes and rolls down her white ankle socks. He wades out into the water, stepping gingerly as if on coals, yelping softly, reaching for her hand. They bump hips. She giggles. His name is Lincoln, and hers is Evie. Upstream from them, sitting on the edge of a bridge over the river, is a thirteen-year-old boy (called Junior by his friends) who gazes at them, annoyed by their exuberance. He grasps a bamboo pole, attached to a red-and-white bobber and drop line. He has a coffee can full of dirt and worms for bait close to his right knee. So far he's caught nothing. Behind him, cars drive over the narrow bridge on their way to the park, rattling the oak planks.

The O'Hara family arrived here thirty minutes ago. The mother has already set up a red checkered plastic tablecloth, while her husband, at the grill, squirts fluid over a heap of coals. Their two children, Barbara, who is three and is watched over by the dog, and Keith, six, have strayed toward the playground. They've been instructed to stay safely within sight. Mrs. O'Hara counts out the tuna-salad sandwiches and the deviled eggs under her breath. The movement of wind traced through an elm stops her, and she sniffs the air. She is lost for two seconds and keeps her eyes tightly closed. No one sees her do this. Then she opens her eyes and begins to count the cookies, separating them into three groups.

For many of these people, the only image of heaven they have ever had, that has ever made any sense, is this: a park, summer, a picnic on wooden tables. Good weather.

11:23. Barbara O'Hara has wandered down to the river. The dog, a female German shepherd named Taffy, watches her. The dog acts, has always acted, as a nanny. She pads along on the child's left and nudges her away from the Huron. From birth, this child has been protected (from stairs, strangers, and rushing water) by this dog.

Lincoln has rolled up his sleeves and is picking up stones from the riverbed and skipping them on the water's surface. Granite, gneiss, a small flat piece of feldspar: the feldspar skips three times before it sinks with a sideways fluttering motion into the water.

This place would not be what it is unless it had a carload of noisy eighteen-year-olds. They are here: Carl, Carl's baby-faced cousin Bob, Bob's next-door neighbor Boone, who wears a pair of glasses with white tape over one lens, and D.F. The four of them have just stumbled their way out of Boone's gray pickup truck. They've left the portable stereo box locked in the cab and are carrying their beers and inner tubes toward the river. Bob and D.F. graduated from high school just last month; the other two have been working for a year now. All four are barefoot and sport T-shirts and cut-off jeans. Barbara O'Hara hears them and scrambles out of their way, followed by Taffy, who starts to growl. As soon as they reach the water they begin splashing each other; unprovoked, D.F. hits Bob in the arm just below the shoulder, and there is a moment of water wrestling before Bob drops his six-pack of Miller Lite and the fight is halted. Carl and Boone take off their shirts; they both have thin, pale chests. Now they drop their inner tubes into the water and sit down, their legs dangling out. Floating downstream, past Lincoln and Evie, who have just kissed, Carl says, All riiiight! and Bob offers Lincoln a beer as he goes by. Lincoln smiles and says no thanks as he shakes his head.

This river is no wider than a residential city street. At this point its rate of flow is approximately fifty feet per minute. Named by the French, it refers to a confederation of four tribes of Indians who lived east of here, all of whom spoke an Iroquoian language.

———

Another family, the Sinclairs, sets up a complicated lunch. This group includes three children, their parents, the paternal grandmother, and two maternal aunts who are not on speaking terms this particular day. The oldest child, Matt, has brought a football and plays catch with his father, while the two aunts silently take lunch out of the hamper. Mrs. Sinclair, having seen Taffy, the German shepherd, ties their mongrel terrier, Jesse, to the leg of the picnic table. The grandmother sits in a folding chair, touching her gray hair and mumbling commentary. Sometimes people listen to her; at other times they just don't. At the moment she is reminiscing about her life as a child, and a park she once visited in Alabama with her Uncle Tyrone, a park that looked like this, where she ate an orange.

Measured from the horizon line, the sun is at an angle of 84 degrees. The wind speed has decreased to five miles an hour. The cirrus clouds, overhead an hour ago, are now near the east horizon.

Just past noon, Junior can smell hamburgers frying on the O'Hara's grill, and hot dogs cooking over a fire that Mr. Sinclair has started. The river itself smells faintly of iron and clay. From another family's grill, thirty feet away, comes the smell of barbecue sauce. This family, the Bakers, have two children. One of them, a very noisy girl, Cynthia, is begging her mother for a piece of Hubba Bubba gum. Cynthia has a catalog model's face, with two registers, for begging and smug contentment. The other child, Donald, is retarded, with short hair, a sloping Down's-syndrome forehead, slanted eyes, and elongated jaw structure. He sits calmly on the picnic bench staring toward the river while his father spreads his homemade barbecue sauce over the chicken with a little brush. As he stares at the water, Donald opens his mouth, showing crooked teeth. His eyes are a brilliant blue.

Over on the baseball diamond a team from the Dexter A-1 Appliance Store has arrived and is warming up for the game that they are scheduled to play against a team from Groh's Chevrolet. Only one member of the Groh's Chevy team has arrived. This person suspects that the others are getting loaded at Shelley Davidson's house, in Dexter.

> *A prayer, a pledge of grace or gratitude*
> *A devout offering to the god of summer, Sunday, and*
>   *plenitude.*
> *The Sunday people are looking at hope itself.*
>
> —Delmore Schwartz,
> "Seurat's Sunday Afternoon Along the Seine"

Junior grabs his bamboo pole and lifts it, yanking the bobber out of the water. The line drips and twitches. Hauling in the fish with the motion of a man pulling at a garden hose, Junior examines his catch, a shiny half-pound sunfish, the size of a man's hand, wiggling in midair and glittering in the sunlight. He reaches out and feels the fish's life flapping between his fingers. After loosening the hook, Junior stuns the fish against the boards of the bridge, then puts it on a green nylon stringer. He attaches his end of the stringer to a corroded nail in the bridge and drops the other end, looped around the gills of the sunfish, into the water.

Lincoln and Evie have waded out of the river, getting their trouser cuffs wet, and are walking back to Lincoln's orange CJ-7. 1:00. They remove a blue cotton blanket and a brown wicker picnic basket from the Jeep's rear cargo area and then stroll away from everyone else, down a narrow path through the cottonwoods, Scotch pine, star thistle, and bur oak.

———

Now along the river there appears a bearded man, dressed in an absentminded and haphazard way, without food or blanket, who sits by himself. His name is Rolfe. He strokes his mustache and beard, as a little girl accompanied by a German shepherd walks past him. In his right hand he holds a book, a new translation of the poetry of Rilke. He unlaces his shoes. Something about the day keeps him from opening the book immediately, perhaps the noise of the children behind him, or the sight of two lovers retreating into the woods, holding a blanket and a picnic basket with their outer hands, holding each other with the inner ones. Rolfe tugs morosely at his beard. He exhales quickly, twice. He looks like a man who has spent most of his life by himself. Behind his glasses the wells under his eyes have darkened from sleeplessness. Feeling dampness seeping through his trousers, he opens his book and begins to read, moving his lips as he always does when he reads poetry, following the words in an inaudible murmur.

Grandmother Sinclair comes waddling down toward the water, keeping up a private monologue about her childhood in Alabama. She almost stumbles against Rolfe but at the last moment changes course and heads east. Her grandson, Matt, is sent down to fetch her.

Cynthia Baker is at the playground, climbing up the steps of the slide, blowing pink bubbles with the Hubba Bubba gum that she has cadged from her mother. She has to wait halfway up for Keith O'Hara, who stands at the top making wide-angle gestures he has learned from Saturday-morning superhero shows. Now he slides down, facing the wrong way. Cynthia sits down at the top, checks to see who's watching her, blows an aromatic bubble, and pushes herself down. As she slides, the bubble pops against her face, sticking to her cheeks.

———

1:30. Stratocumulus clouds appear in the west, moving visibly across the sky in a straight-edged line. For the first time today, a cloud covers the sun. But the cloud continues to move eastward, and the sun reappears. The temperature is 81. The barometer has dropped to 29.32. The wind speed has increased to seven miles an hour, blowing from the northwest.

The four guys—Carl, Bob, Boone, and D.F.—can be heard in the distance, returning to Boone's truck, their voices heavy and excited. Boone and Carl have gone through five beers apiece and are bragging about their encounters with women. Carl is saying, You don't know her, man, not like *I* know her, and the way she talks, man, you know, like real low, shit, I could listen to that *all day*. All night, I mean. She ever whisper to you, man? You know, with her mouth right up there in your ear? Carl laughs once, a conqueror's laugh, and Boone looks suddenly angry, but then he spits and says, She never put none of her mouth in *your* ear, she'd be afraid to, with all them bugs flying out. Carl grins, hooks his finger to his ear, and all four of them laugh. Carl and D.F. have latent pink sunburns on their chests from today's exposure; during the week they work on the line in the Ford factory in Saline. Bob and Boone work outdoors for the highway department. Their bodies have a kind of sallow tan, pocked with blisters.

Mrs. O'Hara, Eugenia, has her family seated, and her husband, Roger, says grace: Bless O Lord these thy gifts which we are about to receive from Christ our Lord, Amen. When the prayer is over, Barbara and Keith look up and begin eating their sandwiches. Taffy, the gray-eyed German shepherd, is lying underneath the picnic table, waiting for Barbara to start throwing down pieces of the tuna sandwich to her. Already the dog's tail is wagging in anticipation, and as she pants she begins, slightly, to slobber.

The softball team from Groh's Chevrolet has arrived in Bart's van, and although they do not look sober, the four women and five men are determined to play ball. They whoop, pat each other on the back, and whistle as they warm up. They give off a powerful smell of hops. The team from Dexter A-1 Appliance cannot believe their good luck, that they're facing nine people who are very seriously in the bag.

Measured from the horizon, the sun now stands at an angle of 75 degrees. More broken clouds appear in the sky from the west, greater in thickness, some with dark centers. With these clouds passing in front of the sun, the effect is that of someone hitting an outdoor light switch.

Lincoln and Evie have placed their blue blanket, which Evie received free from a bank for opening a passbook savings account, at the south edge of the park, a section overgrown with wild cucumber, cow parsnip, Norway spruce, and red oak. They are protected from observers on all four sides. Lincoln has taken off his shirt, and Evie is applying 6-12 mosquito repellent to his back. His skin smells of paint; all week he works at Bill Lee's AMC auto body shop, pounding, painting, sanding, and stripping. Evie is a clerk in the office. No matter how much Lincoln washes himself off, he still smells of the job. When he kisses Evie, she inhales his work, seeded into his skin. She doesn't know yet if she minds it.

Junior, with adult patience, is still sitting on the bridge, having by now caught three fish, including a smallmouth bass. The sun, two hours ago shining on his cap, is now heating up his neck. He looks at the park, yawns, picks up his stringer of fish, and decides to bicycle home.

A huge piece of tuna sandwich falls under the table; Taffy lunges at it.

Look! There's a man, middle-aged, clearing his throat, short-sleeved cotton shirt and white cotton pants, yellow straw hat, walking along the river, accompanied by a raccoon! Not on a leash! Just walking there! People come up to him, look at the raccoon, ask him questions. He shrugs, smiles, keeps walking.

The four guys have brought their portable stereo blaster, a box of cold mushroom-and-pepperoni pizza, and Frisbee down close to the water. They've turned on the radio, loud, to WRIF, self-proclaimed "home of rock 'n' roll," and they are opening more beers, smoking weed, laughing, and stumbling around. Carl makes a comic noise designed to sound like a pig at the trough. D.F. and Bob go off to toss the Frisbee, and Carl sneaks down the river to talk to a girl he's spotted. Boone looks as though he's about to fall asleep. He removes his glasses, separates a slice of cold pizza from the others in the box, and has a bite.

Grandma Sinclair is quiet, eating. Matt and LaVerna glance up at her and wonder how long it'll take for her to doze off. Jesse, the dog, is asleep on his leash in the shade of an elm. His legs pump fiercely: in his dream he follows the scent of a furry rodent into a meadow, and there he pounces on it, picking it up by the neck. Mrs. Sinclair begins to cut a watermelon for dessert, and Matt looks around to see if anyone is going to notice him, out here, eating a watermelon. He hates eating watermelon in public, in a setting like this.

Mrs. Baker has cut up Donald's barbecued chicken for him into little pieces on his white paper plate. Donald, his mouth open, holds his fork in his left hand and spears the pieces; he makes faint vocal sounds whenever he misses. When he is finished, his mother tells him to wipe off his face with his napkin. He smiles, picks up the napkin, and removes the barbecue sauce from his chin. A tiny piece of bubble gum is still stuck to his sister's check. Donald asks why Cynthia doesn't have to wipe that off, and his mother says that she does. Cynthia says, Oh, Mom, and begins with violent exaggeration to pull at her face with a paper towel.

Now, at 2:30, I am here, too, with my wife and son. They've walked down to the water pump, to work the handle, listen to it creak, and put their hands in the cold water as it comes, at last, gushing out. Perhaps they will drink the water, taste its heavy mineral content. I'm lying here on the grass in the shade, some distance downstream from everyone else, dozing off for a moment.

In the second inning, Groh's Chevrolet is at bat, Dexter A-1 Appliance in the field. A small woman, a showroom salesperson, is at bat. As in a game of opposites, a huge man who delivers refrigerators and other such items for Dexter A-1 is playing first base. The woman swings, hits the ball toward left field, and begins running toward the huge first baseman.

Rolfe looks up from his book, his eyes slightly wet. He has been distracted by the radio, by its blare, the noise of music he hates, Ted Nugent, Van Halen, and now the Romantics. Hey, he says, turn that down. The music makes him think of shouting, accidents, cultural anarchy. More loudly he says, Hey, it's too loud. Boone, who is next to the radio, finishing the slice of pizza, doesn't hear him. Rolfe starts to get up. The goddamn radio is spoiling everything.

————

The Bakers, the Sinclairs, and the O'Haras have all noticed the noise of the radio. They've been looking at each other with irritated glances and shrugs.

Clouds have masked the sun, and the wind seems to have died away. Grandma Sinclair looks at the sky, sniffs, and says, I do think it will rain. She shakes her head. What a pity. Spoiling a beautiful Sunday.

Closing his book and lighting up a Pall Mall he has drawn from his shirt pocket, Rolfe feels his hands tremble with anger and anxiety. He places the book he has been reading inside the sleeve of his jacket, which is lying next to him on the grass, and he stands up, brushing pebbles and twigs off the seat of his pants. He stares righteously at the boy eating pizza and listening to the radio. A ruined life, ruining other lives! After taking a long drag from his cigarette, Rolfe walks over to the boy, who gives off a plaguey smell of body odor, marijuana, and beer. Excuse me, Rolfe says, the cigarette in his tremulous left hand, his right hand tugging at his beard. Excuse me, he says, in his classroom voice, more loudly. Boone, who has been lying on his back with his mouth wide open, blinks his eyes and looks blearily at Rolfe. Boone is blind in one eye; its stationary iris is a milky brown. The noise bothers me, Rolfe says, it's bothering all of us. Could you please lower the volume? Boone closes his mouth, stares at Rolfe, then in an efficient gesture reaches over and flips a switch, turning the radio off. Sure, man, Boone says. No problem. It was keepin' me awake anyhow. Thank you, Rolfe says, amazed at the ease of what has just happened, as he returns to his spot by the river. In the sudden quiet he sits down and stares into the water. There is some noise from the softball diamond, but it is distant, muted.

———

Tanya, the saleswoman from Groh's Chevrolet, has collided with the first baseman, and she is lying on the ground, her eyes shut tight, holding on to her leg. Everyone is crowded around her. Jesus Mary and Joseph, the first baseman says over and over again. Jesus Mary and Joseph. One man with muttonchop sideburns rushes off to the park headquarters to get them to notify the emergency paramedics. A woman who knows some first aid covers Tanya's leg. It might be a break, she says. Don't move. Tanya opens her eyes and says, I don't think it broke. I got the wind knocked out of me. And my ankle, I twisted it.

As I doze off, I think about all the people here, the beautiful random motion of everyone taking the day off, and for an instant I think of fitting them into some kind of story. But it's impossible. There is no story here.

Lincoln and Evie have been holding and fondling each other for almost an hour now. With some of their clothes still on, they begin to make love. Lincoln's thrusts are slow and gentle. He intends this as a demonstration: that lovemaking can be recreational, and that, despite his occupation, he has enough tenderness to last lifetimes. At first Evie is afraid of being observed, but gradually she loses herself. She loves it, she loves him. Oh, she says, looking up at the clouds blocking the sun. Oh my God.

The sunlight, the soaring trees and the Seine
Are as a great net in which Seurat seeks to seize and hold
All living being in a parade and promenade of mild, calm
*   happiness:*
The river, quivering, silver blue under the light's variety
Is almost motionless.

—Delmore Schwartz,
"Seurat's Sunday Afternoon Along the Seine"

Now, at this late midpoint of the afternoon, when almost everyone has eaten, walked, and played, the people here seem to slow down, almost to freeze in time. Barbara O'Hara has fed Taffy her last cookie and is lying with her head against the dog's chest, under the picnic table. Keith O'Hara is playing catch with his father, and Eugenia is cleaning up, wondering if she might be able to take a quick nap. Grandma Sinclair is asleep and snoring softly in her aluminum-tubing-and-plastic folding chair, and another one of the Sinclairs, Matt's other sister, Carmen, is leaning against the trunk of an ash tree, awake but not moving. Mr. Baker, Donald's father, still sits at the picnic table, but his eyes are closed, and his head jerks backward every time he starts to fall asleep. Boone is asleep in the sudden quiet of his radio. I myself have dozed off. Rolfe is not asleep—he has both daytime and nighttime insomnia—but, still by himself, he is staring off into the distance, looking at nothing in particular. He throws his cigarette butt into the river. It hisses, then begins to float downstream at a rate of approximately fifty feet per minute.

D.F. and Bob return from playing Frisbee, Carl comes back with a phone number tucked in his pocket, and the three of them wake up Boone. Come on, Ogre, they say, let's move. Feeling the onset of hangover, the four of them pick up their things, load them into the back of Boone's truck, and leave to buy more beer, before settling down at Bob's place, where they will watch tonight's Detroit Tigers game on Bob's father's twenty-four-inch Sony color set. Jack Morris is slated to be on the mound, against Texas.

Lincoln lifts his hips, as a warmth spreads from his thighs up through his buttocks, and comes into Evie. Straddling him, she has both hands at the side of his head, and now she kisses him hard, feeling herself joining an orgasm. It does not matter to her or to Lincoln that she might become pregnant. She has no fear of this man whose skin smells of paint.

First a siren, and then the clatter of oak planks as an Emergency Medical Service ambulance crosses the bridge, enters the park, and stops at the softball diamond. The paramedics remove a stretcher and load Tanya into the back of the vehicle, while everyone who is down by the river and still awake stands up and squints to see what is going on over there. The back doors of the ambulance are closed, and the two attendants get in at the front. The light atop the vehicle's cab flashes on, and the ambulance rushes out of the park to the hospital, where X-rays will be taken, and it will be discovered that she has sustained no fractures but has bruised her muscles and tendons. Behind her, the two teams call off their game and sit in small groups on the grass and the hoods of their cars, talking about other calamities: falls from ladders while putting up storm windows, falls on icy sidewalks, traffic accidents, drownings in four feet of water, heart attacks, strokes, cancers.

Evie lifts herself up to see over the top of the staghorn sumac blocking the view from where she and Lincoln have just finished their lovemaking to the playing field. No, Lincoln says, putting his hands on her shoulders. Don't look. It's nothing. It's not important. Somebody probably just got a little hurt.

As the ambulance heads out of the park, the Sinclair's terrier, Jesse, wakes up and begins to bark, but in a sleepy, absentminded way.

Hooray! Cynthia Baker says loudly. Look! The sun's out again! Her brother, mother, and father look up in the direction where she is pointing a dirty index finger. The cumulus clouds, now at 4:14, have parted, and the sun's reappearance, as if commanded by Cynthia's grating voice, has scattered the mosquitos, gnats, and sand flies that have started to swarm around those who have not kept moving. Rolfe adjusts his glasses and watches a swarm of gnats move collectively down the river, two feet above the surface of the water, a small spherical cloud of flying dots. He rolls up his pants and steps into the river, bending down to examine the sedimentary rocks near his feet. Shale, slate, limestone, lignite, gypsum. One stone in particular catches his attention. He rolls up his sleeve and picks it out. It looks like an arrowhead, but only by accident.

The Potawatomi Indians, who once lived here, part of the larger Algonquian group, were pushed during the late-eighteenth-century migrations into this area from the south and west by the more warlike Sioux. The Potawatomis were a largely agrarian people; for the most part, they grew corn, fished, and hunted. Among their tribal rituals was a festival of the sun. They were the last group of any race whatever living in this area to worship the earth.

There's that man again, walking the other way with that raccoon. The animal has been walking a long time and is panting.

Measured from the horizon, the sun is now at an angle of 30 degrees. The barometer is steady at 29.27. The humidity is 54 percent. The temperature is 81 degrees Fahrenheit.

Here are some people arriving: an enormous ruddy fat man wearing bib overalls but no shirt, followed by his gray-haired wife, who has two watches on her left wrist and a thick copper bracelet for arthritis on her right. She clutches a two-week-old issue of *People* magazine. Two women, Cheryl and Lee Anne, have spread out a blanket in the area recently vacated by the four guys. They open a thermos and drink hot Darjeeling tea from ceramic cups. Another couple, quite young, with modified punk hairstyles, come wading down the river from the west and continue until they are out of sight to the east. They are speaking Dutch. An old man wearing purple suspenders shambles toward the river with a pipe in his mouth, the aroma of the smoke unmistakably that of Cherry Blend. His woolly eyebrows are enormous and extend half an inch on either side of his face. The Bakers, however, are packing up and leaving, as are the Sinclairs. The O'Haras, first to arrive here this morning, will stay for another twenty minutes.

My wife and son and I are about to leave. For an instant I glance at all the other people here and try to fix them into a scene of stationary, luminous repose, as if under glass, in which they would be given an instant of formal visual precision, without reference to who they are as people. Even now, with the light changing, the sun moving more rapidly toward the horizon and the light gradually acquiring that slightly unnatural peach tint it has before twilight when the shadows are grotesquely elongated, I cannot do it. These people keep moving out and away from the neat visual pattern I am hoping for. I breathe out, stand up, and walk with my wife and son to the car.

Taffy, the dog, smelling something under the dirt, begins to dig with her front claws. Soon she has a small hole as deep as Barbara's thumb. If she keeps digging, Mr. O'Hara says, she'll get to China. Beneath her in fact is twenty-five miles of the earth's crust, and beneath that a layer of dense rock five to six hundred miles deep, lying on top of an oxide-sulfide zone that in turn rests on the earth's nickel-iron core. Meanwhile, one mile away from Taffy, Evie, lying on the blue passbook blanket next to Lincoln, holds her finger up toward the sky. Sometimes, she says, when I was a little girl, and I was mad at my mom, I'd lie on my back and think of a ladder that would take me up and away from where I was. I couldn't quite figure out where that ladder went, but I didn't care a whole lot. With her eyes still on the sky, she feels Lincoln's face lowering toward hers, and he kisses her. When he lies back again, he says, I remember something from high school science. Mr. Glenn's class. He touches the fingers of his left hand with the index finger of his right. The atmospheric levels. If you climbed that ladder, he says, you'd go up through the troposphere, the stratosphere, the chemosphere, and the ionosphere. But then you wouldn't be able to breathe. He puts his hand over her left breast. So you might as well stay. He feels her nipple tighten under his hand.

Rolfe has mosquito bites on his wrists, neck, and ankles. A horsefly has also bitten him on the back, where he can't reach around to scratch. His pants are damp from the ground. He has read and reread the translation of the tenth elegy. As he holds the book open with his right hand, he scratches his ankles with his left. Feeling hungry, he stops clawing at himself long enough to light up another Pall Mall.

One of the women, Lee Anne, finishes her tea and now takes out a recorder from her bag and begins to play. The piece is a jig, pre-Baroque, English. Cheryl, whose face is hard to see now, in the diminishing light, holds her cup between her hands and looks toward the Huron as her friend plays.

The O'Haras are leaving. Taffy, perceiving this, runs off to the east boundary of the parking lot, squats down, and pees. Keith O'Hara, wearing a Detroit Tigers baseball cap on his head, saunters over to the slide, climbs up, and slides down backward one last time.

The fat man in the bib overalls sits in repose, staring like the Buddha toward the water. In his hand he holds a little transistor radio. He listens to the baseball game, the Tigers against Texas. The game has just started. His wife fans her face with her copy of *People*.

Now, at 8:30, with the sun barely visible through the trees to the west—no, now gone—a few more families arrive for some after-dinner recreation. But once they arrive they seem eager to leave, and they check the sky and complain about how difficult it is to catch softballs and Frisbees at this time of day.

At dusk, a woman wearing a tank top and running shorts jogs through the parking lot on her way to the bridge over the river. Around her waist is a small belt on which hangs a Walkman. Through the earphones she is listening to Mendelssohn's *Italian* Symphony, the first movement.

What a relief it is, sometimes, not to have to tell a story about these people.

The O'Haras have left. Rolfe is putting on his shoes and socks. He is waiting for the evening star. When he sees it, he will put his book under his arm and walk to his Renault. In the meantime, he smokes another cigarette and watches the smoke rise and disperse into the sky. It is as if words are bombarding him inside his mind, tugging at him, pulling his thoughts ferociously into terrible shapes. Feeling a wave of word-nausea, he bends down, picks up the book of Rilke's poetry, and throws it under a bush.

With Evie's blanket gathered under his right arm, Lincoln holds his lover's hand as they walk to his Jeep. They throw their things into the back and get in. After starting the engine, Lincoln turns on the radio, and then Evie takes the fingers of his right hand, as he reaches down to shift into reverse. He backs up out of the parking place, and with Evie's fingers still resting on his, he shifts from reverse into first gear, lets out the clutch pedal, and steers with one hand through the parking lot out past the gates.

And now, with the sun below the horizon, the woman who wears a copper bracelet suddenly grabs her husband on the arm. His great double chin shakes as he turns to her, expecting a stricken look, but she has only lost her balance for a moment, and is smiling.

There: the evening star: Venus. Still pulling at his beard, Rolfe trudges to his automobile. Cheryl, sipping her tea, nods to him as he walks past.

The temperature is down to 74 degrees. A breeze seems to be coming from the north. The man in suspenders, smoking his pipe, stands next to the glowing ashes of the Sinclairs' charcoal fire and says to himself, I don't know why his feet was draggin' that way, I really don't.

At this time, when the loudest noise is that of the crickets and the wash of the river's water over the rocks upstream, the last light silhouettes the birds overhead, those that cluster near picnic grounds and water: redwing blackbirds, grackles, mourning warblers, waterthrush. But now is the time also for the characteristic irregular swoop and flutter of bats, searching for mosquitoes above those areas where the water has pooled and is still.

In these pools, away from the river's current, where vegetation can thrive, the carp come to rest in the dark, swimming through the water ferns, bladderwort, stonewort, and lilies.

The wingbeat, and the pause—half a second, at most—and then the repeated wingbeat, of the bats.

One family, down at the south end of the park, has started a fire to cook a late dinner. From this fire sparks rise into the night sky, bright-red exclamation points, commas, and periods thrown up out of the coals and glowing in the air before disappearing.

The park closes at 11:00. In one hour and thirty minutes it will be Monday, the day of coffee, air hammers, and binding contracts. But now, in the dark, with the ruddy fat man and his wife still sitting there in the bug-infested grass next to the Huron River, with Ernie Harwell doing the play-by-play at the top of the fifth inning, Texas leading the Tigers three to two, it is still Sunday, the day of forgiveness.

ACCLAIM FOR Charles Baxter's

THROUGH THE SAFETY NET

"Baxter is a master of deceptive simplicity. . . . His fiction makes the American universal in ways that are fresh and unforced."
—*Boston Globe*

"A writer in whom reading is believing." —*Elle*

"There are some writers so gifted that even their colleagues agree, really, they should be better known, their books should be best-sellers. At once inventive and meticulous, their work seems to glow with a steady light. . . . One such writer is Charles Baxter."
—*The New York Times Book Review*

"He is a master of what's actual. . . . Only the great chefs know how to combine, as Baxter combines the effects of the senses, the sweet with the sour, the fierce with the cool, the visual with the auditory."
—*Los Angeles Times Book Review*

"A quiet passion ignites Charles Baxter's best work, making his stories glow." —*Detroit Free Press*

"Like Raymond Carver, Baxter has become a master at articulating the quiet confusion of despair, and of suggesting that despair may, at times, be redemptive, but he's entirely his own writer: precise in setting forth his characters' preoccupations."
—Ann Beattie